THE
darkest
night

THE darkest night

WILL SHE FIND STRENGTH IN GOD OR GIVE INTO HER FEAR?

MARIA S. SAKRY

TATE PUBLISHING & *Enterprises*

Published by Tate Publishing & Enterprises, LLC
127 E. Trade Center Terrace | Mustang, Oklahoma 73064 USA
1.888.361.9473 | www.tatepublishing.com

Tate Publishing is committed to excellence in the publishing industry. The company reflects the philosophy established by the founders, based on Psalm 68:11,
"The Lord gave the word and great was the company of those who published it."

Book design copyright © 2008 by Tate Publishing, LLC. All rights reserved.
Cover design by Steven Jeffrey
Interior design by Lynly D. Taylor

Published in the United States of America

ISBN: 978-1-60462-895-1
1. Fiction: General: Romance, Christian   2. Fiction: Psychological

08.03.26

To my family, for their unending love and support.

and

To Kelly and Daniel, for their love, friendship, and insight—all of which guided me through this project.

PROLOGUE

He carefully kept his distance in the black SUV as he followed her car out of the store parking lot and onto the
road. Instead of turning right, like she usually did, she
turned left. He smiled wickedly as he followed. He knew
tonight was going to be the night.

He had been watching her for weeks, figuring out her
schedule and waiting for the right opportunity to act on
his plan. He didn't feel any self-reproach for what he was
about to do. She deserved a punishment for her actions.
She had snubbed him one too many times, never giving
him a chance to show her how much he cared. She would
be sorry.

Sweat began to drip down his face. He adjusted the
black facemask and turned the air conditioning on. All
the extra clothing made him quite warm, but it was necessary to add bulkiness to his strong, wiry frame. He didn't
want to risk her finding out who he was, at least not yet.
He slowed down as he watched her pull into the lakeside
parking lot. She shut off the engine, climbed out, and
walked toward the lake. *Stupid girl*, he thought. *Doesn't she
know it's dangerous to walk alone at night?*

A few minutes later, he parked almost thirty yards
away from her car and waited for her to return. He knew
she wouldn't be long now. He got out of his vehicle and
crouched like a lion preparing to pounce on its prey. He
could hear her footsteps approaching as her shoes clicked
on the pavement. When she stopped by her car door,

he knew it was time. He moved swiftly and grabbed her before she even had a chance to react. One hand pressed hard against her mouth and prevented her from screaming while the other held her tight against him. Her body sagged against his as if admitting defeat. He knew she was too weak to fight out of his strong grip.

He threw her in the SUV and smiled to himself as he saw her attempt to crawl away from him. *You're not going anywhere, beautiful. I'm going to teach you a lesson tonight that you will never forget.*

CHAPTER 1

April 8, 2003
Duluth, Minnesota

Loneliness spread throughout her body. It engulfed her, suffocating her. She couldn't escape it. An unseen force battled against her very being, seeming to overtake her completely. Mary Canfield fought the tears that threatened to fall beneath the walls of her dark eyelashes. Her weary blue eyes observed the two nurses as they worked to get everything ready. She wanted to believe that this wasn't real, that it was merely a figment of her imagination. She slowly closed her eyes and took a deep breath. *Please be gone*, she silently prayed. *God, please let me be asleep.*

"Mary?" a voice cut into her thoughts.

She hesitantly glanced toward the sound of the gruff male voice that had brought her back to the stark reality of her situation. Officer Schwartz's massive figure filled the entire doorway. His size had intimidated Mary when she had first met him. If it hadn't been for his compassionate brown eyes and gentle words, she never would have let him bring her to the hospital.

"Yes, Officer?"

"I have some good news for you. I got a hold of Stacey. She slept through the first few phone calls, but I was finally able to wake her. I explained you were in trouble and that you needed her here. She promised she would be here shortly. Is there anything else I can get you, or anyone else I can contact?"

"No. Thank you. Thank you for everything." Mary watched as he tipped his hat, turned, and walked away. *How can this be real? How can this be happening to me?* Dizziness swept over her. Her scraped fingers gripped the stainless-steel railing of the hospital bed as she fought to maintain consciousness. She refused to give into her body's weakness. *I need to be strong. Please help me, Lord. I can't do this alone.* Her already pounding heart accelerated as her mind filled with worry. She feared not only Stacey's reaction, but her family's as well. Her large, close-knit family did not take things lightly. She knew this news would devastate them.

Images of her three beautiful sisters—Tracey, Sandra, and Grace—floated through her mind. They had shared everything growing up, and even though there were the normal disagreements that all sisters have, their love and friendship had blossomed with each passing year. A small smile spread across her tear-stained face as she thought next of her two redheaded brothers, Benjamin and Lucas. Their love shined through their endless joking and teasing. The two of them were replaced with the faces of her parents. They had done so much for her and her siblings to show their never-ending love and support.

A fresh round of tears started to stream down her cheeks as Mary thought about how much she missed them and how she wished the night had never happened. She knew they would be disappointed by her lack of judgment.

"Don't cry, Mary. Everything will be all right," an older nurse told her. "We're going to take good care of you here and make sure that you get all the help you need sweetie."

"But my family," Mary sputtered. "They will be so upset with me. It's all my fault. I should have listened. I should have been more careful."

"You can't blame yourself, sweet child. Sometimes things happen in life that you can't control." She paused slightly as she watched Mary touch the cross hanging around her slender neck. "God is the only one in control."

"Then why didn't He stop this?" she spewed. "He has the control to stop evil, so why does He allow it to continue?"

"Oh, He has the power, but He gave us humans a free will. Some of us choose freely to follow Him, and some of us choose freely to turn away. Satan tried to get at you tonight through an evil man's actions. He wants you to blame God and turn away. You can't let him win, so instead you should lean on God.

"He knows your pain and suffering," the nurse continued, "better than anyone else. He suffered and bled for your sins and for that man's sins. That evil man that hurt you doesn't deserve your forgiveness, but neither do you deserve Christ's forgiveness. This may seem crazy to you, but the best way to deal with what happened is to forgive that man and continue to seek God. He may not have stopped what happened tonight, but He did protect you. He did not leave you alone nor will He ever leave you alone. Tonight could have been much worse, but the good Lord has plans for you, child." The kind nurse turned to leave.

"Wait. Why should I forgive him? Does that mean

that his actions should just go unpunished, and I should forget about the whole thing?"

"Something like this isn't easily forgotten, but if you forgive him, in your heart you are moving on. He no longer has a hold on you. He already took one night of your life. Do you want to allow his memory to haunt you any more than that?"

"No, I suppose not. I do understand what you mean about forgiving him. How do you know so much about this?" Mary asked softly, studying the woman's bright green eyes.

"It took me thirty years to forgive the man who did that to me. Forgiveness is freedom, sweetie," she finished and lightly squeezed Mary's hand. "Forgiveness is freedom."

Stacey Hartman rushed around her bedroom trying to find her car keys. She needed to stay calm, but her mind was frantic. She didn't know what had happened to Mary or why she was in the hospital. All the officer had told her was that Mary was at St. Luke's Hospital because she had been involved in some sort of incident. A glimpse of silver under a pile of papers caught her eye. She grabbed the keys and ran out the door.

She drove the abandoned streets to the hospital like a mad woman. *How could there be an incident at three o'clock in the morning? Was she in a car accident? Is she okay?* She wished the officer had been a little bit more specific. Mary was her best friend. She didn't know what she would do if something really bad had happened to her.

Stacey parked her car on the street across from the hospital and ran to the emergency room entrance. Stopping at the front desk for a moment, she checked to see where Mary was.

"Can I help you?" the lady asked.

"Yes. I need to see Mary Canfield. She was brought—" Stacey began.

"Are you Stacey?" a man's voice interrupted her.

Spinning around, she saw a policeman sitting in the waiting area. "Yes, I am Stacey."

"I'm Officer Schwartz. I took the call involving your friend. If you could please sit down, I'll briefly explain the situation."

Stacey's mouth dropped open as she listened to what the officer was saying. After he finished, she sat there stunned, letting her mind comprehend the reality of his words.

"Miss, are you okay?" he asked her.

"Wh...where is she?" she managed to choke out.

He led her to where Mary was. As she stepped into the room, her eyes locked with Mary's. Without a moment of hesitation, she rushed to her friend's side and embraced her. She could feel Mary's body shake as she held her close. Stacey's face became wet as tears steadily made their way down her cheeks.

"I love you so much, Mary. I'm just glad you are okay."

"I know, me too. I'll be fine. I will not let what happened tonight poison the rest of my life," she stated, forcing a brave smile onto her trembling lips as she remembered the nurse's words. "Thank you so much for coming down here. You were the only person I could think of to call when the officer asked. Stacey, I'm so scared. How am

I going to explain this to my family? How will they ever forgive me? Do you think I should even tell them?"

Stacey stood by the side of her bed and looked at her. "Do you really want to keep something like this from your family?"

"I don't know. It would be so easy not to tell them and just pretend none of this ever happened."

"Mary, this isn't just going to go away. You need to talk about tonight. I will be here anytime you need to talk, and I know there are counselors you can also seek out. Is that going to be enough for you, though? I think you should at least tell your mom."

"I can't just tell her. If I tell her, I have to tell my dad and everyone else. You don't understand. We are so close. Once one person knows, it's only a matter of moments before everyone knows."

"Yes, I see what you are saying, but what about the tests and stuff they are running, and the pills they're pre-scribing? Won't they bill your insurance company? You don't want your parents to find out like that."

"Girls," the young brunette nurse broke in, "you do realize that all of this care is paid for by the state. Nothing will show up on your insurance, Mary. You don't need to tell them. This is something that happened to you, not to them. You do whatever you feel is necessary to deal with this."

"Okay." She sat back on the hospital bed, her mind wandering. Did she really want her family to know the result of her thoughtless actions? It would be so easy to just move on and forget this had ever happened. Could she keep something like this hidden, though, especially from her sisters? As her thoughts continued, the room

Maria S. Sakry

changed around her. The white hospital walls morphed into a light pink. Everyone and everything disappeared as her mind brought her back to the room that would remain forever fixed in her memory.

The walls were the most hideous color Mary had ever seen. She hated the color pink. She had asked her mom so many times why they couldn't just paint over them with a nice shade of blue. Her mom always claimed the room was much too large to repaint, so it remained pink. Two twin beds and a bunk bed were positioned on the hardwood floor of the room. Four dressers lined the far wall next to a huge walk-in closet, and in the middle of the room laid a round, brightly colored rug.

Even though the rug was quite beautiful, Mary or her three sisters never touched it. Tracey, the oldest girl, believed a dark hole hid underneath the rug and had told the other girls all about it. She warned them never to step on it or place any toys on it, or they would be lost forever. The sisters all took that news to heart and would carefully tiptoe along the edge of it to get to their beds so that they wouldn't fall through.

Since Tracey and Sandra were the oldest two, they slept in the twin beds, while Mary and Grace shared the bunk bed. Grace, the youngest, took the lower bunk, and Mary gladly occupied the top where she could be seen and heard by her three sisters.

Bedtime was Mary's favorite time of day. At night her imagination came alive with crazy stories that her sisters loved to hear. The only problem was that Mary thrived on being the center of attention. Her excitement caused her voice to become louder and louder as the story went on. Many times her stories had to come to an abrupt halt when an unhappy parent came knocking on their door.

Tonight, though, was different than the other nights. She couldn't risk the chance of their parents ruining their fun. She had to remember to keep her voice down. It was Tracey's last night sharing a room with the three of them, and Mary wanted it to be a night that would always be remembered.

She looked at the expectant faces of her three sisters and began to speak. "As you all know, tonight is the last night we will all be together, so it is time for our good friend Ante to say goodbye as well. Ante, the large ant that has lived in our attic, not only has battled the evil beings that tried to get us at night and comforted us when we were scared, but has also completed his mission. I talked to him tonight and found out he was leaving. When I asked him why, he explained to me that he was no longer needed."

"We still need Ante. He can't go," protested Grace.

"No, we don't. Ante was a part of all four of us, so how can he remain here when one of us is gone? He formed a bond between us that can never be broken. Whenever we think about him, it will remind us of each other and the secrets we've shared and will share, not only as sisters, but as best friends."

"Mary? Hello? Are you still with us?" Stacey's frantic voice cut through her thoughts.

Mary looked at Stacey's worried face and nodded her head. "I'm fine. I just realized what I have to do. I have to tell them."

Maria S. Sakry

"Are you sure?" Stacey questioned as her brown eyes searched Mary's face.

"Yes. I need them, Stace."

She nodded her head in agreement. "I think you're making the right choice. We will call them when we get back to your apartment."

"You'll really stay with me while I call?"

"I'll stay as long as you need me."

"Thank you."

"Mary, we're finally ready to begin your examination. I'm sorry it has taken so long to get everything ready. Just relax. Everything will be okay." The blonde, chubby doctor gave her hand a light pat before lifting the hospital gown and beginning her task.

Closing her eyes, Mary pretended she was somewhere else, anywhere else. She could almost smell the crisp winter air and hear the voices of the people she loved most in the world. Almost.

CHAPTER 2

A white blanket of snow covered the enormous evergreen trees. Mary shivered as she watched the snowflakes continue to fall. The white winter wonderland transformed around her as sawdust and branches started to cover the ground. She bent down, picked up another piece of wood, and handed it to her older sister Sandra.

Every Saturday, as far back as Mary could remember, had been spent in the solitude of the country woodlands. Her father dropped the trees, her brother Ben split them, and the rest of the family worked together as a team to load the cherry red pickup that they used to haul the logs home. At their home the wood was separated into two piles. They used one pile of wood to heat the Canfield home, and the other pile was sold to Mr. Canfield's business associates. The profit from this wood was then used to take family vacations.

Ben, the oldest, loved teasing his younger siblings. His favorite was Mary. He could always get the best reaction out of her. He watched as she struggled to lift a huge piece of wood onto the truck.

"Ugh," she grunted as she heaved it onto the tailgate.

"Look at those spaghetti arms," Ben teased.

"What, these big pipes? They could beat your butt any day," Mary scoffed back. "Why don't you get to work, lazy, and stop supervising?"

Ben let out a hearty laugh. "Okay, crazy old, whatever you say."

"Crazy old?" she questioned.

"Yep, that's right. Crazy old Maurice. That is what I'm going to call you from now on."

"You can't. I'm telling Dad. That is not my name. Dad!"

James Canfield stopped filling the chainsaw with gas and turned toward them. "What's the problem, crazy old?"

Mary screamed. "You can't make fun of me. You are the dad. Dads can't go along with their obnoxious, tree-trunk sons!"

"Tree trunk?" Ben questioned.

Mary turned to glare at her brother. "Yes, if I am crazy old, then you are a tree trunk."

Mr. Canfield laughed. "Okay, it's time to get back to work, you two. We need to get this load done, then we'll go up for lunch."

Ben smirked as Mary picked up another piece. "Fine," she huffed, "but I am not crazy old."

Maybe Ben is right. Maybe I am crazy, Mary thought as the doctor continued her examination. *I must be if I would go to the lake alone at night. But I always do. It's not like tonight was the first time.* She shook her head. *It could have been so much worse. I could be dead. Lord, thank you for keeping me safe and being with me. Please help me and my family make it through this.*

"Mary," the doctor's voice cut into her prayer, "I'm done with the exam. I'll get these samples tested. The nurse will be back in with a pill for you to take that will negate any possible pregnancy, as well as the proper medications to prevent some common STDs and HIV. As soon as you have taken them, you are free to get dressed and go home."

"Okay. Thank you." Her gaze wandered around the room while she waited for the doctor to return with the pills. Her mouth fell open as she caught a glimpse of the clock and realized it was almost five o'clock in the morning. "I can't believe it's that late, Stace."

"Don't you mean that early? I guess we won't be making it to class today."

"No, probably not," she replied. Mary hated missing class, but she knew she wouldn't be able to sit through any lectures today. It was hard to believe that their sophomore year of college was almost over. *What a great way to end the year*, she thought bitterly. She glanced at Stacey and noticed the dark circles under her eyes. "Are you sure you want to stay with me while I call my family and stuff? I understand if you want to get home to bed."

"I'll stay with you, Mary. Don't worry. Everything will be fine."

Mary leaned back and nodded her head. A few minutes later the doctor came back with the medication and a glass of water. Mary swallowed the pills and waited for everyone to leave the room so she could get dressed. Her gray sweatshirt and blue jeans hung on her thin frame. She ran her fingers through her short brown hair and took a deep breath. She could do this. She was going to be just fine. She walked out of the room and found Stacey waiting by the door.

"Let's go home," she told Mary.

Home, she thought. She wished she could go home to her parents' house, but unfortunately, it took three hours to get there. The smells and sounds of that place

Maria S. Sakry

had always comforted Mary. She followed Stacey to her cobalt Monte Carlo and collapsed into the passenger seat. Her eyelids began to droop as exhaustion overtook her. Within seconds she was fast asleep. Her dreams filled with the sweetness and craziness of home.

Tall oak trees lined the chain-link fence like soldiers protecting the white, two-story house. The flowerbeds—full of tulips, pansies, daffodils, and daisies—painted the yard with color. The morning dew glistened on each blade of grass that made up the lush, green lawn, which seemed to go on for miles. It extended past the north end of the house, past the barn, and up to the woods at the edge of the Canfield property. It was the perfect setting for a child's imagination to run wild.

Eight pairs of bare feet crushed the wet grass as they ran. They scurried past the cows in the barn toward the woods. The six Canfield children—along with their two cousins, Lily and Brent—spent every waking moment of every summer vacation outside. Laughter and squeals of delight filled the air as they raced each other to their magical place amongst the trees. To most people the woods appeared to be an ordinary place, but to these children the woods transformed before their very eyes into a town that belonged only to them.

Since it was their first day out of school, a lot of work needed to be done in Teepee Town. They scattered throughout the woods, each going to their own teepee to replace any fallen branches or to rebuild if it had collapsed during the winter.

After Tracey, Ben, and Brent had finished with their homes, they grabbed rakes from the side of the barn and started to rake away the leaves covering the ground. It wasn't long before the leaves outlined dirt paths for the children to ride their bikes on. These paths led all over their little town. Each teepee had a road to it, but there were also roads that led to the gas station, the restaurant, and the Little Boutique shop.

While Mary, Sandra, and Lily worked on moving logs to make seating at the restaurant, the two youngest, Grace and Lucas, went around scavenging for old corncobs and crab apples to use as their food. They continued working through the morning until they could no longer ignore the grumbling in their stomachs.

"Let's go to lunch at the Mall of America today," Tracey suggested.

"Yeah!" everyone yelled in unison.

"We'll have to ride there, since it's so far away," Sandra added. They all agreed and hurried to the shed by the barn to grab their bikes. The pedals moved vigorously as they rode toward the front steps of the house. Huffing and puffing, they climbed the steps and dashed through the front door.

"Welcome to the Mall of America. Wash your hands before you sit down. Clean hands are required to eat at the Mall," Lorraine Canfield reminded them playfully, since she knew all about their games of make-believe. By the time they had reached their seats, they had clean hands and plates full of macaroni and cheese and peanut butter and jelly sandwiches. "Don't eat yet. We still need to pray."

Eight little voices joined hers as they prayed their lunch prayer. "Thank you for the world so sweet. Thank you for the food we eat. Thank you for the birds that sing; thank you, God, for everything. Amen."

The food disappeared as if by magic as the hungry children ate their fill. "You are the best cook ever, Mom," Lucas stated as he put his cup and fork by the sink.

"Thank you, dear." She grabbed a wet washcloth and wiped at his cheese-covered chin. "Did you get any of the food in your mouth or just on your face?"

"I don't know, but my tummy is full. So the food must have gotten in there."

Lorraine chuckled at her four-year-old child's explanation. "Yes, I believe you are right. Okay, time for your nap, young man. The rest of you can either take a nap or play outside."

"We'll play outside," Ben announced as he led the others toward the door.

She watched them head out the door and smiled. Being a mother of six was a lot of work, but it was also a lot of fun. There was never a dull moment, that was for sure. She took Lucas by the hand and led him upstairs to his bedroom. "Mom, can you sing to me? Please, just one song."

"Okay, but first you need to lie down and close your eyes." Once he was situated, she rubbed his back and sang. "You are my sunshine, my only sunshine. You make me happy when skies are gray. You'll never know, dear, how much I love you. Please don't take my sunshine away." His deep breathing filled the room as she stopped singing. Lorraine gently kissed his cheek and left the room.

Meanwhile the rest of the children continued to spruce up their town. Ben looked through the woods for a log to use in his teepee as a couch for company to use. As he bent over to begin rolling one toward his home, a flash of black and white caught his eye. "There's a cow out!" he yelled to his sisters and cousins as he sprinted back into the town. "Grace, you go get Mom, and the rest of us will surround it and drive it back toward the barn."

The children all sprang to action with Ben and Brent leading the way. They spotted the cow eating leaves off a nearby tree. "Okay, make a straight line with only a few feet between each person and slowly walk," Ben instructed. The cow moved away from the tree and started running. The kids chased after it. They watched as the cow jumped through the fence into the fenced-in barnyard.

"We did it!" they all cheered.

"No, we didn't. It jumped in with the big cows instead of going back in with the little cows. Stupid cow," Ben muttered. "I'll take off a few of these boards that separate the two pastures, so maybe we can get him to jump out of this one into the right one." He diligently worked with the hammer, pulling out nails to open up the fence line. "All right, let's get him through this space."

The children cautiously stepped through the pasture to avoid the piles of manure that covered the ground. They lined up behind the calf and walked toward it, but instead of it jumping through the hole in the fence, it just circled in front of it.

"Now what do we do?" Tracey asked impatiently.

"I know," eight-year-old Mary piped up. "I'll be right back." She scrambled over the fence and hurried to the tin shed. She picked up the old garden hose that she had noticed earlier and ran back to the pasture. She tied a knot in the hose to create a lasso and hopped back over the fence.

Maria S. Sakry

"What is that for?" Lily asked.

"Well, you guys, I'm going to throw this over the calf's neck and then pull him through the hole into his own pasture."

"You're going to lasso a cow?" Ben laughed. "Where are we, the Wild West?"

"Laugh all you want, but you'll be apologizing to me when I get the cow back where it belongs." Mary neared the scared cow and carefully swung the hose so it landed around its neck. She smiled triumphantly at her older brother. Now all she needed to do was pull the cow through the opening. As she tugged on the hose, though, the cow reared up and took off in the opposite direction. Its unexpected actions caught her off guard as the hose slipped through her fingers. Falling, she landed in the ankle-deep manure face first.

Her brother, sisters, and cousins howled with laughter at the sight of her. "Good idea, smarty pants," Ben and Brent called to her.

"What in the world are you children doing?" Mrs. Canfield stood with her hands on her hips and stared at Mary as she got up out of the cow poop.

"A little cow got out, Mom, and we sent Grace to go get you for help," Ben explained.

"I know all that. I saw Grace sitting in the backyard playing with the kittens all alone. I went out and asked her if something was wrong. She told me what happened, but that still does not explain why Mary is covered in poop."

"I'm sorry, Mom. I had a great idea about how to get the cow in the right pen. The thing is, though, that cow had a different idea. Maybe next time I should talk to it, so it knows which way to run."

It was useless. Mrs. Canfield could not stop the grin that quickly spread across her face. A snort escaped as she tried to control her laughter. The contagious giggles that spilled out of her caused the children to laugh uncontrollably. The little cow stared at them as if they had all gone completely mad. "All right, let's get this cow back where it belongs. Lily and Sandra, go help Mary get washed off. You can use the hose in the backyard."

"Make sure she doesn't try to make a lasso with it," Tracey joked. Another round of laughter filled the air. Once they were finally able to settle down, Mrs. Canfield positioned Ben, Brent, and Tracey behind the cow. She slowly walked over to the calf and stayed close while it gradually strode to the fence. Without any effort it leaped through the opening back to where it belonged. Ben hurriedly replaced the boards and then circled the fence looking for where it had gotten out in the first place. At the back of the pasture, he found the hole and patched it up to prevent any further escapes.

"Good teamwork, everyone," Mrs. Canfield told them. "How about we celebrate with some ice cream cones?"

"Yeah!" they all agreed.

"Let's go. I think we've had enough fun for one day."

"I don't want to smell like cow poop anymore. I hate cows," Mary mumbled.

"What are you talking about? Mary, wake up." Stacey softly nudged her shoulder. "We're here at your apartment. You can go back to sleep after we call your parents."

Mary sat up and blinked her eyes. The first rays of sunlight were just beginning to touch the darkened earth. She marveled at God's breathtaking masterpiece. Hues of red, orange, pink, and yellow filled the morning sky as God moved His paintbrush across His vast canvas. It amazed her that He could transform the darkness of night into such a bright and beautiful morning. *That is what I do to your heart when you forgive*, a voice seemed to speak to her. *Your bitterness and hate are replaced with peace and love.*

I know, Lord, Mary silently prayed as she got out of the car and followed Stacey up the steps to her apartment. *I want to forgive him. I want to move on from this. I need to, so I can be strong for my family. I forgive him, God. I forgive him for what he took from me. Even though he ran away with my innocence, he can never take you from me. Heal me, Lord, and heal him. Help him turn from his evil ways and find you.* A calming peace settled over Mary. All her stress and worries melted away like snow on a warm spring day. She unlocked her apartment and held the door open so Stacey could go in first.

Once their shoes were off, they plopped down on opposite ends of the tan leather couch. Stacey scrutinized Mary's face. "Something is different about you. Are you okay? Are you sure can handle calling your parents? Maybe you should lie down first."

"Stacey, I'm going to be okay. Actually, I'm going to be more than okay. This nurse talked to me when I was waiting for you to arrive. She reminded me of God's amazing gift of forgiveness, so just a few moments ago I forgave the man that did this to me. I know it might sound ridiculous, but I've never felt more at peace. I'm sure there will be a lot of tough moments and days to come, but I know that God will never forsake me. He'll hold my hand and walk with me every step of the way."

CHAPTER 3

Getting ready for school, Mrs. Canfield, Lucas, and Grace hurried through the house early Friday morning. Mr. Canfield stood by the stove and observed them as he cooked breakfast. A smile of amusement tugged at his lips as he watched them run around like chickens with their heads cut off. He flipped the strips of bacon with pride because he knew they rushed to have time to eat the delicious breakfast he prepared.

Lucas, a sophomore, and Grace, a junior at the local high school, had to leave the house by quarter to seven to make it in time to Youth for Christ. They were both Christians and thoroughly enjoyed the hour of fellowship, prayer, and worship with their classmates. Grace had just finished pinning up her dark brown hair when Lucas joined her in the bathroom. She smirked as she watched him try to get a comb through his bushy red hair.

"Well, good morning, Napoleon. How was your sleep?" she teased.

He caught her eye in the mirror and snorted. "My hair isn't getting that bad, is it?"

"Heck yes, it is. You're such a nerd."

"Really, I'm a nerd? Have you ever seen a nerd with abs like this?" he asked as he lifted up his black t-shirt.

Grace's dimples appeared as she smiled at her brother. "Oh, get over yourself and get ready. Mom wants to leave soon. She has a student coming in early to make up a test."

She brushed past him and slid into her chair at the kitchen table.

In the other end of the house, Mrs. Canfield curled the last piece of her hair. Putting the curling iron down, she ran her fingers through the silky red strands. She stepped back and took a final look in the mirror. Her sparkling blue eyes and cheerful expression made her appear years younger than her age of fifty-one. Satisfied with her reflection, she left the bedroom and headed for the kitchen.

Appetizing aromas of scrambling eggs and sizzling bacon filled the air while loud country music blared from the CD player on the counter. She snuggled up behind her husband and put her arms around his waist. "Good morning, honey."

"Well, good morning. You look pretty today." He lowered his balding head as he kissed her lips.

"Get a room," Lucas called to them. "Seriously, I'm trying to eat here."

The husband and wife stared at each other and grinned. Mr. Canfield winked at his wife and kissed her again. "Can I have this dance?"

"Of course," she answered.

He spun her around and pulled her close as their feet moved to the country beat. Their love had only grown over the past twenty-six years of marriage. Lucas and Grace looked at each other and snickered. They had always teased their parents about their shows of affection, but, truthfully, they were happy. They knew they would rather see their parents kissing than fighting.

Just before the song finished, the phone began to ring. "Grace, turn the radio down, please," Lorraine told her daughter as she stopped dancing and picked up the cord-less. "Hello."

"Mom, this is Mary. Something happened last night ... " she broke off as she started to cry.

Lorraine's smile instantly disappeared. "Mary, what happened? You better tell me right now." She nervously glanced at James. "Did you do something to your father's car?"

"No, Mom. I ... I was raped last night." Mary cried.

Lorraine's hand clenched the phone. "Oh, Mary, how did this happen?"

Tears began to roll down her porcelain cheeks while she listened to Mary's explanation. James placed his hand on his wife's arm and gave it a comforting squeeze. "Why would you go down there alone at night? Why didn't you listen to our advice and keep yourself safe?"

"I'm so sorry. I know I messed up." Mary continued to weep.

"Yes, you did," her mother's tone softened. "This isn't your fault. You should be able to take walks whenever you want without worrying about someone hurting you." Another round of tears filled her eyes. "Oh, Mary, I just can't believe this happened to you. Thinking about what you had to endure sickens me. Why couldn't you just listen? I can't handle this right now. I have to get to school. Bye." Mrs. Canfield hung up the phone and sobbed into her husband's chest.

Shocked, Mary stared at her phone, unable to believe that her mother had just cut her off. Stacey reached over and hugged her as she cried. Gut-wrenching sobs filled the apartment. "Why ... why did she just hang up? Didn't she know that I needed to talk to her more? Maybe I … I shouldn't have called."

"Mary, none of this is your fault. I even heard your mom say so. She knows that despicable man is to blame. She's just really upset and doesn't know how to deal with it."

"Maybe, I just—" Her words stopped abruptly when her cell phone began to ring. "It's them." She took a deep breath and answered. "Hello."

"Mary, this is Dad."

"Hi," she softly replied. She braced herself for a lecture. *Please help me, Lord. I need you. Help them see that this is truly not my fault. Help them realize that I'm going to be all right.*

"Hun, your mother didn't mean to be so abrupt. She's just upset and angry that this happened to you. We all are. Please don't take her words to heart. She doesn't blame you. We just love you so much that the thought of you being hurt is unbearable. We are so thankful that you're alive. God must have known we still needed you here," his soothing voice cracked with emotion.

Another round of tears filled her blue eyes, but this time they were tears of happiness. God had just answered her prayer in a matter of seconds. They still loved her. Hope filled her spirit and lifted her heart. "I love you guys." She sniffled.

"We love you too, and nothing could ever change that. How are you doing? Do you need us up there, or do you want to come home?" he asked, his words laced with concern.

"I'm doing okay. I'm not really up for driving home, but you could come up here if you want. I know you probably need to cut wood tomorrow, so it's not a big deal if you can't."

"Crazy old, the wood isn't going anywhere. We'll head up as soon as your mom gets out of school."

Hearing her nickname brought a smile to her lips. It lit up her tearstained face like the sun shining through the clouds after a storm. They were going to make it through this. Their love, laughter, and faith would help them overcome this obstacle like they had overcome so many others. "Thanks, Dad."

"No problem. We'll see you soon. Go get some sleep."

Once they said their goodbyes and hung up, Mary rested her head in her hands. She felt drained, as if all her energy had been sucked out of her. "Thanks for staying with me, Stace. That was the hardest thing I ever had to do."

"I understand." Her arms enveloped her and squeezed her tight. "I'm really proud of you." Stacey released her and bent down to put her shoes on. "I should get going, but remember—I'm only a phone call away if you need anything." After she left, Mary slipped beneath the white sheets of her bed and fell into a deep, dreamless sleep.

Stacey tiptoed into her bedroom and quietly shut the door. She couldn't wait to climb into bed and go back to sleep. She stripped off her blue sweatshirt and pulled the ponytail out of her curly blonde hair.

"Where have you been?" an angry voice greeted her.

She spun around to find her boyfriend perched on her bed. He watched her like a hawk as she stepped toward him. "What are you doing here?" Surprise was etched all over her face.

"Well, I came over to check on you when you didn't answer any of my phone calls. I was worried, but obviously you're fine." He stood and paced the room. "Look, Stace, if you're seeing someone else, let me know and I'll leave. I will not be played a fool."

She quickly closed the space between them and gazed into his baby blue eyes. "I love you, Clint. I never want to be with anyone else. I'm sorry I missed your calls, but something unexpected came up." She cleared her throat. "I wasn't out seeing some guy. I was with Mary."

"You were with Mary? Why? Was she upset about something?" A peculiar expression flickered across his face.

That was strange. For a second, it almost looked like he was amused by the idea, she thought. "Yes, something happened last night." She watched to see if the expression would return; instead, concern filled every feature of his face. *I must be seeing things. I really need to get to bed.* She shook the thoughts from her mind and continued, "Some guy raped Mary last night, so I went to the hospital to comfort her."

"Oh, Stacey, I'm so sorry for accusing you. I feel horrible. Is she okay? Is she still in the hospital? Do you want to go back and see her?" The words tumbled out of his mouth.

"No, she is home safe in bed now. She called the cops after it happened, and they brought her to the hospital. She only suffered a few scrapes and bruises, but they thought it was vital for her to get checked out. They wanted to attempt to collect any residue that the rapist could have left on or in her body. Once they were done with all that, I drove her home and then headed back here." She lowered herself to the bed and sadly looked up at Clint. "Physically she's okay, but I'm kind of scared about her emotional wellbeing."

Her eyebrows knitted together as confusion set in. "She blames herself for what happened, yet she seems so peaceful and calm. I'm just afraid she's going to wake up and start freaking out. I mean, all she wants to do is move forward from the incident. I just think she might be moving a little quick. She's already forgiven the guy who did this to her, and she keeps talking about how amazing God is. I just don't understand." Stacey lay back and stared up at the ceiling as if she could find the answers there.

Clint stretched out his tall body next to hers and ran his index finger along her jaw. "She'll be okay, Stace. If that is her way to deal with it, just let her. All we can do is be here for her when she needs us." He lightly brushed his lips against hers and pulled her close.

She knew he was right. Besides, she was too tired to worry about it anymore. She'd call her tomorrow and check up on her. Her worries and fears vanished as she gave into her fatigue and fell fast asleep.

Trent Jacobson slammed the hood of the '71 stingray corvette shut and jumped behind the wheel. "Come on, baby, start." A grin spread across his grease-streaked face as he heard the engine purr to life. A powerful roar echoed off the tin walls as his black leather boot stepped hard on the gas. He quickly double-checked the gauges before letting off. Positive that everything was in order, he turned the key and climbed out. He knew the owner would be impressed with the speed and quality of his service.

He arrogantly whipped a comb from the back pocket

of his faded jeans and ran it through his wavy black hair. Intense green eyes scanned the messy countertops of the garage for his cell phone. His striking looks caught the attention of any girl he wanted, except for the one that really mattered. He refused to think about her, though. It didn't matter that her sapphire eyes haunted him every second of every day. He ignored them just like he ignored anything else that reminded him of her. Glimpsing red underneath a pile of papers, he pushed them aside and picked up his cell.

He flipped it open and saw he had missed two calls while he was working. *Maybe she called. Nope. I don't even know why I bother getting my hopes up. Hmm, Ben called though; that's kind of weird. We just talked yesterday,* he thought. *Maybe he changed his mind about going out tonight.* He dialed his voicemail and waited. "Hey, Trent, this is Ben. I have some bad news. Mary was raped last night. My parents just called me, but I'm down in Minneapolis right now working. I can't get back to Duluth until Sunday, so I was wondering if you could go over and check on her, and just make sure she's doing okay. My parents should be there around six or seven, but I'm just scared for her. If you could be a pal and go check on her, I'd really appreciate it. Thanks, man. Talk to you later. Bye." Trent angrily gripped the phone.

He paced the garage, his long strides eating up the cement as he walked. He tried to maintain control of his emotions. He wanted to rush over to her, but would she want him there? After all, she hadn't called to tell him— her brother had. She was also the one that had broken up with him two months ago. He had loved her, and she had just thrown him away. *But maybe if I show up there, she will see how much I still care,* he thought. *Maybe she'll want me back.*

Without another second of hesitation, Trent snapped his phone shut and closed his shop down. After locking all the doors, he hopped on his bike and sped off. The motorcycle weaved wildly in and out of traffic as he drove to the woman who held his heart in the palm of her hand.

CHAPTER 4

Mary groggily climbed out of bed and went into the bathroom. She gasped as she stared at her reflection. Her beautiful face had distorted into a pale, splotchy mess. Dark circles under her eyes and ratted brown hair added to the hideous appearance. She glanced at the mirror to see if it would break from her ugliness. When it remained intact, she removed her clothes and jumped in the shower. *Hopefully this will help. I don't want to scare my parents,* she thought as she scrubbed her hair.

Twenty minutes later she felt like a new woman. With a white, fluffy towel wrapped around her tightly, she examined herself in the reflective glass. "Not bad," she commented. She noticed the dark circles were still there, but makeup would take care of that. She ran a comb through the wet tangles and parted her hair in such a way that the short tendrils framed her oval face.

She took out her mascara and began applying it to her long lashes. A loud pounding noise interrupted her routine. Startled by the sound, she dropped the tube of makeup in the sink and placed a hand over her rapidly beating heart. *Calm down. It's probably just Stacey checking up on me.* Replacing her towel with a fluffy, white robe, she unlocked the door and cautiously opened it. "Trent?"

He stared openmouthed at the woman before him. His eyes traveled up from her toes and rested on her eyes. He never knew a vulnerable woman could look so attractive.

He opened his mouth to speak, but the words would not come.

Mary, remembering her manners, slowly stepped aside to let him in. "Please have a seat, and I'll be right back." She walked back to her room in a trance. *Why is he here? What does he want from me?* She grabbed a pair of sweatpants and a t-shirt and quickly put them on. *Maybe he knows about last night and wants to cheer me up? But how could he know?* Her thoughts followed her back to the living room.

He sat on the edge of the brown recliner and waited for her to sit down. "Mary, I'm sorry for just barging in like this, but I had to see you. I had to see that you were okay. Ben called me earlier and told me what happened. I just thought you could use a friend." He joined her on the couch and gave her a quick hug.

"Thank you, Trent. That was very sweet of you." She returned his hug.

He reached inside his leather jacket and pulled out a plastic bag.

Mary looked at it with curious eyes. "What's that?"

"Open it. I hope it cheers you up."

Untying the bag slowly, she glanced at him again. When the bag fell opened, she saw what he had brought her. She lifted up the bag of Milky Ways and the DVD of *Napoleon Dynamite* and smiled at him. "I can't believe you remembered my two favorite things. Thank you, Trent, this really means a lot."

"You're welcome. Do you want me to stay with you? We could watch it together and get fat eating all this chocolate." He gave her a pleading look. "Please, I don't think it's a good idea for you to be alone."

"Thank you for being such a good friend. I haven't been alone, though. God has been with me through it all. He reminded me how to forgive and promised that He'd never leave me."

His back stiffened at the mention of God. He angrily pushed away from her and stood up. "Why do you have to do that? Why do you always have to talk about that?"

"Trent, stop."

"No. I'm so sick of hearing about God. If anything, I thought this experience would have shown you that God doesn't exist. He can't exist because a real God would never have let such a horrible thing happen to a person like you."

"Trent—"

"I'm not finished. Did you know that I love you? I do. I love you. I never stopped loving you, even when you broke up with me because of my lack of beliefs. I'm sorry if I'm not the perfect mold of what you had in mind, but one thing is for sure. You'll never find a love greater than mine." He marched furiously to the door and opened it. Whipping around, he glared at her and snarled. "I would have done anything to prove my love to you."

The words vibrated in her mind as he slammed the door shut. Appalled at his dramatic behavior, she shook her head. She couldn't believe the drastic change in him. He had been so sweet when he showed up, but as soon as she mentioned the G-word, he had turned into a psycho nutcase. She didn't understand it. She had never met anyone so against God. Maybe she shouldn't have brought up God, but she couldn't help it. The words had just flowed off her tongue.

I don't know what to do about him, Lord. He's acting so

strange. I didn't mean to make him mad. And maybe he does love me, but he could never love me more than you. I could never choose him over you, Jesus. Sighing, she locked the door and headed back to her bedroom. Her eye caught the picture of her family. She wondered if her parents were close. She reached for her phone to call them when it started to ring. Mary glanced at the caller ID and answered softly. "Hello?" A long pause followed her words. "Sandra, are you there?" She could hear her sister crying and sniffling.

"Mary, are you okay? Why didn't you call and tell me?" Sandra blubbered.

Tears pooled in her eyes. "I'm sorry. I figured Mom and Dad would tell you guys. After I called them, I just couldn't call anyone else. It was too hard."

"I understand. I'm so glad you're okay. Can we come up and see you? I know Mom and Dad are driving up there tonight, but Tracey, Grace, and I want to come up tomorrow if that's okay."

"I would love that. What about the boys? I want to see them too."

"I think Ben and Lucas plan on coming up on Sunday, so that way we get our sister time." She took a deep breath and continued. "You're so lucky, Mar, that you made it out alive. He could have killed you. I couldn't believe it when Dad called me. I cried forever. Then I called Tracey, and we cried even more. I never knew a person could cry so much in one day."

Mary dabbed the corner of her eye with a Kleenex. "I know exactly what you mean. I love you. You guys coming up here means everything to me. I don't know what I'd do without you."

"Me either. I can't wait to see you tomorrow. Call if

you need anything at all. If you need to talk or cry, I'll be here. Love you."

"Love you too. Bye." Mary clicked off and blew her nose. Her family was coming. The decision to tell them had been one of the best decisions she had ever made. She could have made it through this without them, but she didn't want to. She needed them. Their love and support were going to help her heal ten times faster than if she had gone without it. She leaned back against the headboard and thanked God for the best family in the world.

James slowly pulled into the parking lot of Mary's apartment and glanced at his wife. She nervously tapped her fingers on her thighs. "Are you ready for this, Lorraine?" he inquired as he parked the maroon suburban in the visitor lot.

"I'll feel a lot better once I see her," she replied as she met his gaze. "I just never thought this would happen to one of our kids. I'm scared for her."

"I know, me too. Just remember—this isn't her fault, and it isn't our fault. It just happened, and at least she's alive to tell us about it. All we can do is love her."

"You're right. Let's go up and see our girl." Lorraine reached for her bag and got out of the vehicle. James did the same. They walked side by side up to the apartment. James knocked once and waited in silence with his wife. Seconds later the door flung open to reveal their daughter alive and well.

"Mom, Dad, I'm so happy to see you." She leaped into their open arms and hugged them tightly. She never wanted to let go. She felt so safe and protected in their loving arms. "Thank you so much for coming." She held on to them a moment longer then stepped back. "You can put your things over there. Do you want anything to eat or drink?"

"No, Mary. We're fine. Why don't we sit down over here, and you can tell us the whole story," he motioned toward the couch.

"Okay." As soon as they were all seated, she began to tell them about the night before. She explained everything that had happened. She cried at some parts, but she pushed through. She didn't leave anything out. She even told them about the nurse and her talk with God. When she finished, her parents' damp eyes matched her own.

Her father removed his glasses and wiped at his eyes with the back of his hand. "So will they be able to find this guy? Do you have any idea who it could have been?"

"I couldn't see the man at all, like I said, but they might have found something on me at the hospital. The police also asked me if the man seemed familiar to me, like if I knew him. I told them that I was too upset to really tell. They think it was probably just some random guy waiting for someone to come along."

She searched their faces and noticed the worry in their eyes. "I'm fine now. That man took one night from me; he could have taken my life. God protected me, though, and brought me back to you. He didn't do that so I could waste my life wallowing in self-pity. He did that so I could fulfill His purpose and follow Him."

Love replaced the worry as they gaped at the amazing young woman before them. Her wise words touched their hearts and filled their spirits with peace. They knew Mary was in good hands.

Maria S. Sakry

CHAPTER 5

That stupid girl! He slammed his fist into the wall. This wasn't how it was supposed to be. She was supposed to be depressed and angry. Instead, she was thanking God and forgiving rapists.

She forgave me. His evil laugh filled the room. *I wonder if she would be so forgiving if she knew who I was. Maybe I'll have to pay her another visit.* He knew he would have to wait awhile. He could wait. He was a very patient man when he wanted to be. He would plan the perfect opportunity to strike. This time, though, he wouldn't leave her alive.

He popped open a can of beer and took a long swig. As the cold fluid ran through him, he felt himself begin to relax for the first time in days. He finished the can in minutes and reached for another. Changing his mind, he put it back and reached for his brown jacket. *Forget drinking alone.* He needed to get out. He needed to socialize.

He strutted toward the door, then quickly turned around. He had almost forgotten. He followed the hall back to his bedroom and stepped into his walk-in closet. He carefully parted the clothes and sneered as he stared.

Hundreds of pictures of Mary covered every inch of the wall. All the pictures he had taken when she thought she was alone. He had worked hard to get these pictures. He needed them all, and he still needed more. Seeing her was a necessity. He couldn't live without seeing her beautiful face. He gently kissed his fingers and placed them on her paper lips. "Goodnight, Mary. I'll be seeing you soon."

Maria S. Sakry

CHAPTER 6

March 16, 2006
White Bear Lake, Minnesota

The clear, blue waves of the Pacific Ocean crashed upon the island's sandy shore. A warm breeze blew through her long, brown hair as she watched it from the spacious deck of her beach house. She inhaled the salty air and sighed contently. Her gaze wandered from the water to a lone figure coming up the beach.

His piercing blue eyes met hers as he strolled towards her. She couldn't tear her eyes away from him. Transfixed, her body refused to move as he ascended the wooden steps. She knew she couldn't possibly know this man, but she felt like she did.

He gently took her hand in his, placed his other hand on her lower back, and began to move. Never taking her eyes from his, she moved with him. A soft, soothing melody floated through the air as they danced. She didn't know if it was real or simply a melody of her own heart. She did know that she had never felt like this with anyone. She had been waiting so long for the right man to come into her life. Maybe she wouldn't have to wait anymore.

He opened his mouth to speak, but instead of words, only barking came out. Confused, she tried to step back, but he held on to her tightly. Before she could escape, he lowered his head and kissed her. Any feelings of love were quickly replaced with disgust as he slobbered all over her face.

Mary awoke with a start. "Sick! Maverick, how many times do I have to tell you that I don't like morning kisses from you?" Innocent brown eyes stared back at her. "Do you want to sleep outside from now on?" The Great Dane lowered his head and whimpered. "I didn't think so, now come on. I'll get you something to eat." He barked with approval and followed her into the kitchen.

After she gave him food and water, she glanced at the stove clock. The bright red numbers read 7:50 a.m. "What? Are you kidding me?" She ran down the hall back to her bedroom and threw off her pajama pants and tank top. She couldn't believe she had overslept again. This was the third time this week. What was her problem?

Deep down, she knew. She had known for a while, but she figured if she denied it long enough, it would eventually go away like it had the previous two years. Last night's note had really shaken her, though. The hateful, vulgar words scrawled on the piece of paper didn't seem real. She didn't want them to be real because they scared her.

Lord, help me please or I'll never make it through the day. I need a verse. She scanned the sticky notes stuck to her desk. *Where is the one that Grace sent me? There it is.* She reached for it and quickly skimmed the lines of Isaiah 51:12–14:

> I, even I, am He, Who comforts you. Who are you that you are afraid of a man who dies? Why are you afraid of the sons of men who are made like grass, that you have forgotten the Lord Who made you? He spread out the heavens and put the earth in its place. Why do you live in fear all day long because of the anger of the one who makes

it hard for you as he makes ready to destroy? But where is his anger? The one in chains will soon be set free, and will not die in prison. And he will always have enough bread.

Help me make it through the day without fear. I want to serve you, not fear him, she prayed. Knowing she had no time to shower, she tugged on a pair of blue cargo pants and a white collared shirt. Pulling her long hair up into a messy bun, she raced to the front door, slipped on her black boots, and grabbed her keys. Quickly locking the quaint, yellow house up, Mary jogged to her silver Accord and hopped in.

Derek Elstrom impatiently tapped his foot as he listened to the manager of White Bear Lake EMS rant and rave about some Mary girl. This was not how he had pictured his first day as a paramedic. At twenty-four, he had dreamt about this moment his entire life. There had been a few setbacks, but he had pushed through and finally finished his schooling. He didn't want to be inside right now waiting for a girl; he wanted to be out there saving lives. He let out an exasperated sigh. *Women,* he thought.

Just then the door of the station banged open as Mary rushed in. The flush in her cheeks and brightness in her eyes were both dead giveaways that she had been running. Gawking, Derek's breath caught in his throat. He'd never seen anyone so beautiful. "I'm here. I'm sorry for being late. It'll never happen again. I promise."

"Ms. Canfield, in my office now!" the manager commanded.

"Yes, Mr. Falin," she replied meekly.

Derek forced himself to look away. He didn't need to

complicate anything by staring at her like that. She probably had a boyfriend anyways, and it wasn't like he was looking for anyone right now. He'd found out a while back that women were simply too much work. At this point in his life, he didn't need someone else to worry about. He already had everything he needed. As raised voices leaked through the office door, though, he couldn't help but feel sorry for her. *It's not your problem, so stop thinking about her,* he ordered himself. Standing up, he cleared his mind and stretched out his muscular, six-foot frame.

The office door clicked open and the two emerged from the office. Mary calmly stepped forward and held out her hand. "I'm Mary Canfield. I'm very sorry for being late on your first day. I hope you'll forgive my rude behavior, and we can start over."

Even though her proper manner surprised him, he didn't let it show. He shook her hand and offered a kind smile. "I'd like that. I'm Derek Elstrom, and I'm very happy to meet you."

"Okay, now that you are both here and have been introduced, we can finally put you into the call rotation. Ambulance ten is on a call right now, so you guys will be up next," Mr. Falin informed them. "Mary, show him around and make sure you two do your ambulance check."

"Okay, sir. We will. Let's go, Elstrom, we have work to do," she replied rigidly before she stalked away.

This should be an interesting day, he thought as he hurried to catch up. Especially if she's going to pretend to be an ice princess all day.

"So, Mr. Jacobson, what do you think? Do we have a deal?"

Taking in every angle and space, Trent scanned the four-car garage one last time. He had wanted to expand his business down to the metro area for some time, and now he finally could. He even had a place to live in the area, since his grandpa had just recently passed away and left his house to Trent. He also knew his cousin was quite capable of handling the Duluth shop, so he could spend as much time as he needed down here. He grinned at the real estate agent. "Yes, I believe we do."

"Great, I'll grab the paperwork for you to sign, and then you'll be all set to go." The agent's heels clicked as she walked away.

Alone for the moment, Trent proudly strutted across the cement floor. He couldn't believe this was actually his. All his hard work had definitely paid off.

He wished Mary could see him now. A dark cloud of bitterness settled over him as memories of her came rushing back. He would be paying her a visit very soon, whether she liked it or not. The best part was that she had no idea how close to her he really was. By staying in touch with her brother Ben, he had been able to keep track of her over the past couple of years. He couldn't wait to see her face when he showed up outside her door. He still had a few unresolved issues to discuss with Mary Canfield.

"Here we are. Just sign these, and the property is all yours," the lady interrupted his thoughts.

Trent picked up the pen in his right hand and confidentially signed each document. He could feel the pretty, blonde agent studying him. Never one to pass up an opportunity, he figured he might as well mix some pleasure with his business. "Ms. Stone, since I'm new in town, I was wondering if you'd like to show me around tonight—maybe grab a bite to eat. I do have an errand I need to run, but I'll be done around nine if that works for you."

"Please call me Kim, and I'd love to." The bubbly blonde flipped her hair and flashed him a flirtatious smile. "I'll give you a proper White Bear Lake welcome."

"Okay, she's already completely dilated, and the baby is crowning. We have no time to transport. This baby is coming right now. Let's get her up on the stretcher before we start. Derek, stay next to her and hold her hand or whatever you can do to comfort her," Mary instructed. "Ma'am, I can already see the baby's head. We're going to have to deliver this baby here, then get you to the hospital as quickly as possible."

The lady nodded her head and continued to breathe heavily. Holding onto her tightly, they picked her up and gently laid her on the stretcher. Once she was securely in place, they put a pillow underneath her to lift up the lower region of her body. She bent her knees and spread her legs apart. Her breath quickened, as the contractions became closer and closer together. Feeling the need, she pushed.

Careful to avoid any soft spots, Mary spread her fingers out to support the emerging head. As soon as the head was completely out, she suctioned the mouth and then the nose to clear out the amniotic fluid.

The mother groaned in pain. "I want it out of me! Get it out!"

"You're doing well," Derek soothed her. "One more push, and it'll be out. Don't strain, though. Come on, you can do it. It's almost there."

Making sure not to pull, Mary delicately guided the rest of the body out of the mother. She held the baby on its side, keeping the baby's head slightly lower than the rest of the body, and suctioned the nose and mouth again. She wrapped the screaming baby in a warm, clean towel and handed her to Derek. Clamping off the umbilical cord in two places, she stopped the flow of blood. Once it stopped pulsing completely, she went in between the clamps and cut the cord.

"Congratulations, you have a beautiful baby girl," Derek told the exhausted mother as Mary delivered the placenta and put it in a plastic bag to transport with her.

"You did really well," Mary added. "We're going to get you to the hospital where you'll be a lot more comfortable."

Derek marveled at the miracle he had just been a part of. Not only had he helped a small, helpless baby into the world, but he had also witnessed the deep love and passion in Mary's eyes during the birth. The dull, cold person she had been all day had melted away the moment someone needed her. It baffled him that she could keep such a large part of herself constantly hidden behind a wall of ice. He didn't know why she did this, but he knew that he could help by being her friend. He didn't care if she wanted one or not; she was going to have one. After all, his stubbornness matched hers, and he was determined to chisel all her ice away, even if he had to do it piece by piece.

CHAPTER 7

Derek Elstrom consumed Mary's thoughts on her drive home. Not only did he look like the gorgeous man in her dream, but his kind and compassionate behavior toward her and their patients also appealed to her. This unexpected attraction surprised her greatly; she couldn't remember the last time she ever gave any man a second thought.

She tried to avoid men as much as possible. Besides her dad and brothers, the few she did talk to were men she worked with. Their age or marital status made them seem less threatening, so she befriended them willingly. Derek, on the other hand, had caution written all over him. Even though he seemed nice, she worried that becoming friends with him could lead to something more. She didn't have room in her life for that yet, no matter how much she wanted it. Refusing to feel an ounce of sadness, she pushed Derek from her mind and pulled into her driveway.

Mary trudged through the muddy puddles and melting snow to retrieve her mail from the dented, metal mailbox. She couldn't wait for the snow to be completely gone; she already knew which flowers she would plant all over her front yard. She flipped through the pile of envelopes as she walked back towards the house, *bill, bill, credit card, bill.* She stopped when she reached a large, white envelope. *Not another one? What is this guy's problem?*

Fearing the worst, she sat down on the front steps and opened the letter. She let out a sigh of relief as she pulled out a wedding invitation. She laughed at herself for being so paranoid. Mary had completely forgotten she had asked Grace to send a replacement for the one she had lost. A baby picture of Grace grinned up at her from the front of the invite. She couldn't believe her little sister was getting married in a little over two weeks. A lone tear slid down her cheek, landing on the blue-and-white notice. She was happy for her sister and happy with her own life, but sometimes she longed to have someone too.

Stop being such a baby. At least I have Maverick. Wiping away the tear, she stood up and walked along the edge of the house to the fenced-in backyard. "Maverick! Are you ready to go in?" she called to him. Only silence answered back. She turned on the yard light and scanned the area. The still yard showed no sign of him. "Hmm, that's weird. Where could he be?" Understanding hit her like a bolt of lightening. *I forgot to put him out this morning. I'm such a scatterbrain,* she thought as she unlocked the backdoor and hurried inside.

Unpleasant odors met her nostrils as she walked down the hall. She glanced in her bedroom and grimaced at the damage only a tornado could have created; a tornado named Maverick. Books and papers lay haphazardly all over the floor. A broken antique lamp and toppled nightstand rested among them. Her eyes moved to the bed. Ripped in several places, the white, down comforter hung pathetically off the four-post bed and revealed the source of the stench. Maverick had left her a nice smelly present in the center of her favorite Egyptian cotton sheets.

Disgusted, she shook her head, stepped further into the destruction zone, and paused. The bland porcelain vase her mom had transformed into a realistic country scene lay in a million pieces on the hardwood floor. She wanted to scream or cry, but she knew that it wouldn't do any good to blame the dog for her forgetfulness.

Where is that crazy mutt? Mary left the room and called for him. He barked furiously at the sound of her voice. "Where are you, boy?" As she neared the hall closet, the barking seemed to get louder. *What in the world is he doing in there?* She opened the door and fell backwards as the one hundred and fifty pound Great Dane pounced on top of her.

Showing his utmost gratitude, his saliva-dripping tongue licked every inch of her face. "You're welcome, Mav, now get off!" He gave her one last lick before obeying the command. "Thanks." She patted him on the head as she got to her feet. "Now, how did you get in there?" He barked once and bounded off towards the kitchen.

She followed him into the room and froze when she saw the white envelope hanging on the inside of the front door. She slowly took it down, sliced it open with her fingernail, and pulled out a single sheet of paper. Her body trembled as she read the scrawled words.

I ve been waiting almost three years to feel you again. Maybe I can wait another year, but maybe I can t. Don t worry. Either way I ll be coming for you. It s only a matter of time until you are no one else s but mine.

He had been in her house. Her legs felt like jelly as she wobbled over to the black leather sofa and collapsed. She fought to control her shaking body as sobs escaped her lips. How did he know where she lived? Was this someone's idea of a sick joke? She kicked off her shoes and curled up under the blue, flowered quilt her mom had made for her.

Maria S. Sakry

God, please take this away. I don't know how much more I can handle.

Maverick trotted over to her and jumped up on the sofa. He whimpered and nudged her with his nose. "Lay down, boy." Understanding his master, he stretched out next to her. Mary rubbed his head and cuddled up next to him. *I know I shouldn't fear him, but I'm so afraid. Protect me, Lord. Please keep me safe.* She prayed and cried into Maverick's fur.

He was in my house. He shut Mav up in the closet. What if he's still here? Her blood ran cold at the thought of him lurking around. She needed to call the cops; maybe they would know what to do.

Where is he? He should have been home an hour ago. Her black Jimmy Choo high heels clicked on the marble floor as Stacey paced back and forth in the foyer. Breathtakingly gorgeous in the strapless, black dress, she waited impatiently for the man she had hoped to impress. Headlights flashed the windows. *It's about time. He probably forgot all about our anniversary.* She angrily marched out the door.

She stopped mid-stride when she saw Clint holding a dozen red roses next to a black, stretch limo. Dressed in a black tux and wearing a charming smile, he looked like a prince coming to carry her off into the moonlight. "Are you ready, darling?'

Her anger and resentment disappeared. "Yes, Clint, I am. Thank you so much. I love you." She passionately kissed his lips before climbing into the limo. "Where are you taking me?"

"I am taking you to the finest restaurant in White Bear Lake."

"Bernellies, you remembered our first date." Her eyes sparkled with amusement.

"Is that funny?"

"No. It's a very nice surprise. I just remembered how my nerves got the best of me that night. I didn't know a person could drop their fork five times during one meal." They both chuckled at the memory.

Clint stopped laughing and looked directly into Stacey's eyes. "I have spent four incredible years with you, Stace. I know we've had ups and downs, and I know those will continue to happen. I also know that I would rather spend a hundred bad moments with you than one good moment with anyone else. You're my best friend, Stacey. I never want to lose you. Would you do me the honor of becoming my wife?" He held out the shimmering two-carat diamond ring.

Tears filled her eyes as she stared at the man she had loved for almost four years. She had dreamt about this moment for so long. Everything was just how she had always imagined it. He loved her and wanted to be her husband. A wide grin spread across her face. "Yes, Clint. Yes!"

Derek pushed the button on his answering machine and started to fold his laundry. "Hey man, it's Eric. I was just calling to see how the first day went. Did you save any damsels in distress? Seriously, you need a woman, so if you didn't find one today, I think you should come out with the boys and me tonight to view the local selection. Call me back. Bye." He laughed at his best friend's message. The guy couldn't seem to get a clue that he didn't want a girl right now. An image of Mary delivering the baby flashed through his mind, but he quickly pushed it away.

He put his clothes in his bedroom and wandered around the downstairs of the house he had grown up in. Each room held a memory from his past. He felt restless and lonely as he remembered the good times he used to have here before his parents became sick. His mom had passed away three years ago, and his dad followed a year later. Lung cancer had taken them both. He had given up so much to be with them during the stages of their treatment, but in the end the cancer had won. It had taken his parents and had left him all alone in the world at the age of twenty-two. He knew they were in a better place, but that didn't make the pain any easier to deal with.

He needed to get out. As much as he hated the bar scene, it beat sitting home alone. He grabbed the cordless and punched the familiar numbers. "Hey, Eric, yeah, I'm on my way over." He hurried out of his house and gunned the engine of his beat-up, red Pontiac. Unwanted thoughts weaved through his brain as he weaved in and out of traffic. *You're running away. No I'm not,* he argued back. *I just don't want to be alone.*

As he whipped into Eric's driveway, he noticed all the cop cars at the yellow cottage next door. *What is going on over there?* Curious, he got out of the car and peeked over the shrubs that separated the two properties. A few cops moved in and out of the house while a uniformed cop and a man in a tan trench coat spoke to a woman. Her back faced him, but it seemed oddly familiar. In an instant, she turned and caught his gaze with her own. His heart stopped as her ice blue eyes bore into his. *Mary.*

Before he could speak or wave, she turned back to the

men and continued their conversation. He stood staring at her, unable to decide what to do. She obviously seemed to be well taken care of, but should he go over and make sure? The protector in him wanted to be over there, but she hadn't seemed very happy to see him. As he fought back the urge to hop the bushes and pull her in his arms, he realized the effect this girl had on him. Her intriguing complexities had hooked him somehow. For the first time, he didn't want to run away from a girl; he wanted to help her.

Knowing she needed her space tonight, he forced his feet forward and headed into Eric's house. Tomorrow at work he would talk to her. He would find out what happened and find a way to protect her.

Detective Benson waited for the last officer to leave before joining Mary on the front steps. His heart ached at the sight of this wide-eyed, vulnerable girl. Her dog sat dutifully to her right, so he seated himself to her left.

"They didn't find anything, did they?" she asked, staring straight ahead.

He let out a long sigh. "No, Mary, we didn't. There were no fingerprints on anything in the house, which means the notes are probably clean too. We'll get them checked out though just to make sure. There was also no sign of forced entry, which means he may have a duplicate set of your keys. I suggest you sleep somewhere else tonight and get your locks changed first thing tomorrow morning just to be safe."

"I'll get them changed, but I have to sleep here tonight. I don't have anywhere else to go. All my family is at least an hour away, and my friend Stacey didn't pick up when I called," she explained sadly.

"Normally I don't do this, but I could run you up to your parents' house if you wanted me to."

She sheepishly looked at her hands. "Thank you for the offer, but I can't go there. My sister is getting married in a couple of weeks, and I don't want to freak everyone out, especially if it's just a prank. They have enough stuff to worry about."

He reached into his coat pocket and pulled out the plastic bag with the note in it. After reading it through a few times, he looked over at her. "Do you really think it's just a prank this time? I read through the police reports from last year and the year before. Both years this guy sent you threatening letters for about a month. They started in March and stopped after the first week in April. Is that right?"

She nodded her head in affirmation.

"Okay, and both years nothing happened. His notes proved to be false threats, so the police came to the conclusion that it was simply a prank; someone trying to scare you."

"Yes, that's right, and I agreed with them, but deep down I knew it had to be more than that. When they started coming again at the beginning of the week, I knew it couldn't be a joke. He followed me down here." She covered her face with her hands and began to weep. "Why doesn't he leave me alone? He already hurt me once. I don't want him to hurt me anymore."

"Who did? Who do you think is doing this?"

"The man who … who raped me," she cried.

Instinctively, the detective wrapped his arms around

her and rocked her back and forth. "Shh, Mary, it's going to be okay. I'll call my wife and have her make up the guest room for you. You can even bring the dog with if you want. We'll keep you safe. Don't worry. He's not going to hurt you anymore."

He had watched discreetly through the kitchen window as the mangy dog had led her to the note. At least that dumb dog had been good for something. The dog's unexpected appearance in the house had almost ruined his plan. It had taken all his strength to lock the brute in the closet. He needed to make sure Maverick never interfered again. An evil smile spread across his face as he pictured Mary's horrified expression when she found her dog dead.

"What was that devilish grin for?" asked the woman sitting across from him.

"Hmm? Oh, I was just thinking about how good you look." His reply seemed to satisfy her, so he returned to his thoughts of Mary. He recalled how she had shuddered with fear and collapsed on the couch like a scared little girl. She didn't seem so strong now. The three years of letters were getting to her. Soon she would be weak—weak enough for him to strike.

CHAPTER 8

The Friday morning sun streamed through the large bay window and illuminated his face. Derek blinked awake, sat up slowly, and stretched. Even after late nights, he usually awoke with the sun, as if his body could tell when the last bit of darkness faded away. Still a little tired from the night before, he lazily closed his eyes and yawned. An image of Mary staring at him with those piercing eyes popped into his head.

Jolting his memory, he jumped out of the king-sized bed and headed for the shower. His mind propelled him to move faster as the upcoming conversation with Mary filled his thoughts. He knew his words must be chosen carefully; he didn't want to risk scaring her away. The notion of giving up a friendship or the chance of a relationship with Mary simply wasn't an option. He needed to be patient and cautious with his feelings—for both their sakes. After all, the idea of enduring another broken heart made him wince with pain. The hot water turned into vicious raindrops as his mind traveled back to that unforgettable June day.

Lightening flashed and the thunder, demanding to be heard, rolled loudly across the blackened sky. The rain pelted violently against the windshield as Derek drove Athalia home. He glanced over at his fiancé and smiled. "I love you. I'm sorry we had to cut our date short. You can always come over to my house."

Her lovely face turned into an ugly scowl as she stared at him. "I hope you're joking. I'm sick and tired of being stuck in your house all the time. With your ailing parents there, I feel like I'm constantly at a hospital. You never pay any attention to me; it's all about them and their needs. Why can't they just die already?"

Her callous words stung like a slap across the face. "What? How could you say something like that?" Disbelief filled his face.

"I'm sorry. I shouldn't have said that. It's just that I want the old Derek back, the Derek that used to stay out all night with me and never put me second to anyone."

He whipped onto the long, paved driveway that led up to her parents' house. The dark, brick mansion stood lifeless like a body without a soul. He thought it suited Athalia perfectly, since she obviously lacked the ability to feel. "Get out. I never want to see you again."

His firm, soft-spoken words astonished her. "Fine! I hope you have a nice, lonely life. Once your parents are dead and gone, you'll be sorry for tonight. When you're all alone, you'll be sorry," she shrieked before jumping out of the car.

Derek shook the shrill voice from his head. He never regretted for a second what he had done that night. He may have lost his fiancé, but he found a love far greater than any human could offer. He thought about how his parents had led him to Jesus on the darkest night of his life. His heart would still be broken if it hadn't been for them and for God. Even though he missed them every day, he knew he still had God. *Please help her, Lord, and keep her safe. Give me the words that will help her not harm her,* he prayed as he finished getting ready and headed out the door.

Mary shivered as she groggily awoke from her slumber. She smiled sleepily when she saw both blankets draped over Maverick. "Stealing the covers again? You silly dog, no wonder I'm frozen." She looked around the unfamiliar room and tried to remember where the bathroom was located. Spotting it next to the stairs, she grabbed her clothes and went in. She changed quickly and tied her hair back in a ponytail. Not wanting to disturb anyone, she found a notebook and wrote a short note thanking the detective and his wife for their kindness. She shook Maverick awake, and they silently slipped out the front door.

A warm breeze welcomed her as she stepped outside. Mary closed her eyes and breathed in the delightful scent of spring. Thank goodness she didn't have to work on such a beautiful day. *Maybe we'll head to the park after we get the locks changed,* she thought as she watched Maverick sniff out the ground. "Come on, boy, let's go home." She let him in the Accord's back seat and climbed in.

Where is she? he thought as he looked at the clock for what seemed like the hundredth time. *She can't possibly get away with being late again. I should have stopped at her house and made sure she was awake.* At precisely 8 a.m. the station door opened, but instead of Mary, a short, older man came in. Dressed in blue pants and a white shirt, Derek knew he had to be a paramedic.

The man strode towards him and held out his hand. "I'm Matt Henisson, and you must be the new guy."

"Yes, that would be me. Most people call me Derek, but new guy works."

Matt's lips twitched slightly before breaking out into a huge grin. "I think we're going to get along just fine."

"I think we will." Derek matched his smile. "So you're on the weekend shift?"

"Yes, I am. I usually work the twelve-hour day shifts on Friday, Saturday, Sunday, and Monday, and then I have three days to spend with my wife. It works out nicely. I assume you work the same thing."

"Yep, except I work Thursdays instead of Mondays."

"Ahh, so you've met Mary then." A knowing look crossed his face. "You like her, don't you?"

His face blushed crimson. "Why … why would you say that?"

The old man let out a hearty laugh. "Because you'd have to be blind or stupid not to, and you don't seem to fit either description." He looked closer at his face. "I bet you assumed you would get to work with her today too."

As Derek's blush deepened, Matt's hearty laughter filled the room. "Don't worry. I'm not going to tell, unless you're unhappy about getting stuck with an old man."

"No, I'm glad I get to work with you," he replied quickly.

"Good answer." Matt gave him a friendly smack on the back and started walking towards the sleeping quarters. "Oh, one more thing," he added as he stopped and looked over his shoulder. "If you do anything to harm that girl, you'll be sorry."

Maria S. Sakry

Looking him straight in the eye, he answered earnestly. "I would rather die than see her hurt."

The spotless house gleamed in the sunshine. It had taken her a few hours to get everything cleaned up, but she didn't mind; she loved turning messes into masterpieces. Her family even joked that she suffered from an obsessive-compulsive disorder since she cleaned all the time. Her eyes swept across the house as she walked to the back door. Pleased with her work, she stepped outside and stuck her key in the brand-new lock. *Hopefully these will keep that man out,* she thought. After it clicked in place, she opened Maverick's gate and let him out.

"How does the park sound buddy?"

He barked with approval and stood like a statue as Mary hooked the leash to his black collar. "Good boy. Off we go." Maverick led them down the driveway to the walking path and kept a steady pace as they strolled towards the neighborhood park. She continually glanced around to make sure nothing was out of the ordinary.

Children's laughter filled the air as they neared the park. Two little girls playing in the sandbox smiled up at her as she walked by. Her heart ached, but she ignored it like she always did. She didn't dare wish for something she couldn't have.

Finding an open area of green grass, she turned the beast loose and reached in her shoulder bag for his old, brown baseball. He barked wildly and jumped up as he watched her wind up and throw it. His massive body ran after the tiny ball. He snatched it up in his mouth and brought it back to Mary.

"Hey, cool dog. Can I throw him one?" a boy's voice asked her.

She turned to the boy who looked about thirteen and laughed at his pleading look. "Sure, here you go." She dropped the slime-covered ball in his open hand.

"Cool! This is so cool!" He whipped the ball far out into the grass and jumped with delight when Maverick fetched it and carried it back to him. "Can I do it again?"

"Sure."

"Oh, hold on. I want my friend to watch." He scanned the group of kids on the playground. "Alden! Come over here. I want to show you something." A brown-haired boy jumped down from the monkey bars and started running towards them. Before he could reach them, though, he tripped over his own feet and landed face first on the pavement.

Time seemed to stop. For a moment there was no sound. Then a blood-curdling scream sliced through the air like a knife. Mary saw the blood coming from the boy's mouth as she raced over to him. "Maverick, stay! Somebody call 911!"

Connected by threads of skin, his bottom lip dangled off the left side of his face. He screamed in pain. "Alden, you're going to be okay. My name is Mary. I'm a paramedic, and I'm going to stay with you until the ambulance arrives. Okay?"

He calmed a little bit and gave her a slight nod. Not able to find anything to stop the bleeding, she ripped the sleeve of her shirt off and held it on his mouth. A small crowd gathered around the two of them while they waited for the ambulance. They only had to wait a few moments when two paramedics rushed over to them.

Maria S. Sakry

"Miss, we can take it from here," Derek stopped as he found himself face to face with Mary.

Don't look at him. He saw me last night. He saw the cops. He's going to want answers eventually. Answers I don't have. I'll just talk to him in a normal voice, so he won't know I'm freaking out inside. "He tripped while he was running. His top teeth hit his bottom lip hard and sliced it open," she informed him coolly, then turned to Alden. "You're in good hands. I'm proud of you for being so brave." *There, that wasn't so hard.*

Matt winked at her as he and Derek helped him onto the stretcher. "See you later, Mary. Thanks for all your help." They moved away from the group and headed back to the vehicle.

Oh, I forgot to call Mary back. I can't wait to tell her my news. She's going to be thrilled, Stacey thought as she drove home from work. *I should just stop and see her then I can show her the rock.* She passed Hilton Crest and continued on Century Avenue until she reached Oak Lane. She pulled into Mary's driveway and got out of the car. As she neared the house, she heard a familiar, beautiful alto voice. When she knocked lightly, the singing stopped and Mary answered the door.

"Stacey! What a nice surprise. Come in." Mary gave her a quick hug and let her in. "How are you? It feels like we haven't talked in forever, even though it's only been a week."

She took a seat on the couch. "I know. I do have some news for you, but I have to ask you something first. Were you just singing?"

Mary laughed. "You heard that? Didn't it sound dreadful? Pastor Thomas wants me to sing this song at the youth service on Sunday night, but I don't understand why. I'm sorry if I hurt your ears."

"You're kidding, right? You sounded incredible. When is this thing? I want to see you perform."

Her cheeks blushed slightly. "Thank you, Stace. It's Sunday night at nine, but it's at my church. I know how you feel about church, so I didn't think you'd want to go."

"Of course I want to go. I will get directions from you tomorrow, so Clint and I don't get lost. Speaking of which…" She thrust her left hand in Mary's face. "We're engaged!"

"Oh, Stacey, that's amazing!" she screeched and hugged her best friend. "When did this happen? How did this happen?"

Stacey filled her in about the romantic night. Her eyes sparkled as she told every detail. "We want to get married next May, and I want you to be my maid of honor."

Her face fell at the news. "I think you should choose someone else."

"What? Why?" Baffled, Stacey stared at her friend as if she had grown a second head.

"I don't want you to be upset if I can't make it to the wedding." She walked over to the kitchen counter and began to pace in front of it. "Last night something happened." Mary fumbled over her words as she explained the most recent note. She held back her tears as best she could, but a few still escaped. "I'm really afraid, Stacey. I'm terrified he's going to get me again, but this time I won't make it out alive."

CHAPTER 9

She is not going to get off that easy. Derek pulled into Mary's driveway and contemplated his plan. *I am not leaving until she tells me what is going on.* He shook his head. He didn't understand why women had to be so difficult. Didn't she realize he had spent the entire day thinking of her? He marched up the steps and knocked loudly on the door.

The door swung open to reveal a shocked Mary. Staring wide-eyed at him, she could barely form the words to speak. "De...Derek what are you doing here?" *How can he be here when I look like this?* Taking in his pressed khaki pants and black button down shirt, she sighed and glanced down at her sweats. She wanted to crawl into a hole and die. *Why don't guys call before they come over?*

All his resolve melted away when he looked at the frightened woman before him. *Lord, give me patience. I want to know what is wrong, but I don't want to push her away. Please give me the words,* he prayed quickly before answering. "I'm sorry. I can see I've startled you, and that was never my intent. If you want me to leave I will, but first hear me out. I know something happened last night, and maybe it's none of my business. However, I am your friend, and I want to help." He pulled a brown, wicker basket from behind him and smiled. "I thought a picnic supper might cheer you up."

A small smile touched her lips. "A picnic in the middle of March—isn't it a little chilly for that?"

"It doesn't have to be nice out to have a picnic.

Growing up, my mom took me on countless picnics. Whether it was rain, shine, summer, or winter, she would find someplace to have them. Some picnics took place in a field of tall grass while others were spent on our living room floor. The locations changed, but my mom never did. She used our picnic time to listen to my problems and comfort me the best she could."

"Your mom sounds like a very special woman."

"She was." His face became somber as he handed her the basket. "I'm sorry again for the intrusion. I hope you enjoy the food." He turned to leave.

Was? She must have died. His sadness touched her heart. Impulsively she reached out and lightly touched his shoulder. "Please stay. Eating alone on the floor would be a pretty pitiful sight."

Breaking his serious mood, he let out a laugh. "That's true."

"Hey!" She playfully hit him on the arm.

"Just kidding. You're too beautiful to be pitiful." Before she could respond, he took the basket into the living room and set it down on the blue carpet.

Baffled by his compliment, she followed him and watched as he spread out a red, checkered blanket and unloaded the food from the basket. She smiled widely when she saw the two McDonald's bags. "I'm sorry you had to labor over a hot stove all night to create such a delicacy."

Laughter erupted from his mouth at her words. "I know. I just got off work, so I didn't have time to cook. Do you like cheeseburgers?" He handed her one and took a seat. "I hope you don't mind."

"No, not at all. This is great, Derek, thank you." She

opened up the burger and took a big bite. "Mmm, this is exactly what I needed."

They ate in silence, each alone with their thoughts. On the way over, he had been determined to get answers, but now he sat contently and observed her while she ate. He hoped she would open up to him with time, but he didn't want to rush her. *I have to stop staring or she'll think I'm a weirdo.* He averted his gaze to the black coffee table and noticed the sheet music spread across its surface. "Do you play?"

"I do play piano, but that is actually my vocal music. I'm supposed to sing Sunday night at the White Bear Lake Church of Christ, but I'm absolutely terrified. I know the music, and I've been practicing. However, I suffer from a horrible case of stage fright."

"I'm sure it's not that bad. You'll be fine, especially if you've been practicing." He impulsively reached over and squeezed her hand.

She gently pulled her hand back and studied her fingers before answering. "No, the last time I performed in front of an audience was at my piano recital ten years ago. I'm sitting at the grand piano and start to play the piece I had memorized and practiced at least a hundred times. I get to the middle of the song, and my mind completely blanks. My nerves must have affected my brain because then I stand up in front of two hundred people and tell them I can't remember the rest. I slink back to my seat and listen to the next performer. Halfway through his song, I remember the notes I was supposed to play." She let out a laugh and then frowned. "I don't want that to happen on Sunday because this song is too important. I want this song to reach people."

"Just remember who you're singing to. When you see all those faces staring back at you, remind yourself it is for God, not for them. Pray and He will give you peace. Philippians 4:6–7 states: 'Don't worry about anything; instead, pray about everything. Tell God what you need and thank him for all he has done. If you do this, you'll experience God's peace, which is far more wonderful than the human mind can understand. His peace will guard your hearts and minds as you live in Christ Jesus.'"

Who is this man? she thought as she stared into his kind eyes. *I don't know if he's supposed to be my friend or something more, Lord, but thank you for bringing him into my life. Thank you for reminding me how important prayer is.*

Derek leaned forward, tucked a stray strand of hair behind her ears, and lightly kissed her cheek. "Pray, Mary, and your voice will glorify Him." Standing up, he picked up the trash and headed into the kitchen. "I should get going. I guess I'll see you Thursday at work."

She touched the place where his lips had been. A simple kiss had never felt so intense. *Thursday? Was he crazy? I can't wait almost a whole week just to talk or see him again.* "I'll walk you out." She got to her feet and opened the door. Clearing her throat, she began to speak as they reached his car. "Umm, would you, umm, like to come on Sunday night? I mean, if you're not too busy or tired from work. It starts at nine, so if you can't, I understand."

Amused at her nervousness, he smiled. "I would love to come. I could come over after work, and we could ride together if you want."

"That sounds great. Thank you so much for the food and the company; you really cheered me up." Before she could chicken out, she wrapped her arms around him and gave him a big hug. "You helped more than you know."

"No problem, I'm glad I could be of service to you." He closed his eyes and breathed in the strawberry scent of her hair. Her tall, willowy body fit perfectly in his arms as if it belonged there. He never wanted to let her go, but he had to. He gave her a light squeeze and broke their embrace. "I'm looking forward to Sunday. Remember to pray, and please be safe. Bye, Mary."

"Bye, Derek." She gave him a small wave and walked back to the house. She didn't know how it happened, if it was his actions or his kind words, but somehow Derek had ignited a small flame inside the heart she had carefully protected for so long. Maybe it was time to let someone in, as long as that someone was Derek. She smiled to herself as she thought about his strong arms around her. For a moment, she had felt safe and secure—like nothing could harm her. But now she felt alone. *Pray,* Derek's wise word popped into her head. *Please be with me, Lord. Help me remember that I am never alone and that you can protect me more than any human. Thank you for everything you've done for me. I would be nothing without you. I am nothing without you. Amen.*

Making it difficult to see the curves, the Saturday morning sun reflected off Trent's windshield as he sped towards his new shop. He couldn't wait to get everything set up. He wanted it to be up and running by the end of next week. The sun blinded him for a second as he tried to follow the road. *Stupid sun! Where is the centerline?* A honking horn caused him to veer sharply to the right. Hitting the gravel, his bike threw him off.

He lay still for a moment as his brain attempted to register what had just happened. Groaning softly he slowly sat up, took off his helmet, and looked around. The other vehicle rested in the opposite ditch bank next to a telephone pole. *Oh, please let them be all right.* He brushed himself off and staggered over to get a closer look. "Hello? Are you okay in there?" he yelled to the man behind the wheel.

The man opened the door and got out. "I think so. It just looks like the pole nicked the mirror a little bit. No big deal."

"Are you sure? I can get that fixed for you or give you some money. I feel terrible. I could have killed you."

"Don't worry about it. I know how cruel the sun can be on this road. Besides, we're both fine, so there's no point in making a big fuss about nothing." He extended his hand toward Trent. "I'm Derek Elstrom."

"Trent Jacobson." He shook his hand. "I just moved down here from Duluth. I'm opening a new auto body shop, so I wasn't kidding when I said I could fix the mirror for you."

"That's very kind of you, but I think it gives my baby here her charm." He laughed and slapped him on the back.

"So you don't want anything from me? Nothing at all?" Trent ran his fingers through his hair and sighed. "There must be something you want."

"No, but I do want to invite you somewhere. One of my friends is singing tomorrow night at a church. Since you're new in town, I thought you might like the opportunity to meet some people. It might be safer than running them off the road." Derek gave him a friendly smile.

Trent smirked. "You're probably right." He wasn't a big fan of church. Actually that was an understatement; he loathed the very idea of church. On the other hand, he was kind of lacking in the friend department, and Derek did seem cool. *I guess I could just suck it up for one night.* He sighed loudly. "Well, maybe if I'm not busy, I'll check it out. Where is it at?"

"It starts at nine at the White Bear Lake Church of Christ. Do you need directions? I could have Mary call you."

"No, oddly enough I know where it is. I actually moved in right across the street from it," he answered while the rest of Derek's words soaked in. *Mary.* The name repeated over and over in his head. *It couldn't be her. Could it?*

"Great! That works out perfectly. I guess I'll see you tomorrow. It was very nice meeting you."

"You too. See ya." Trent watched Derek run back to his car. He still couldn't believe he hadn't yelled or demanded money from him. Maybe people were nicer down here. Shrugging his shoulders, he walked back to his bike and picked it up.

Besides a few dents, no other damage had been done. *Mary.* He needed to be careful if it was her. When she saw him, he wanted it to be outside her door, not at a church.

Clint stared at the computer screen in front of him and typed furiously. His boss wanted the proposal by Monday morning, so he would get it done. Late work was unacceptable. He couldn't fall behind schedule or his promotion would be nonexistent—the promotion he needed to help pay for Stacey's ring and their house.

"Hey, honey." Stacey came up behind him and gave him a quick kiss. "How is the work going?"

He took off his glasses and rubbed his tired eyes. "It's going. I should be done with it soon, hopefully. All your interruptions aren't helping though, Stace. What do you need now?"

His impatient tone surprised her. "Nothing. I just wanted to say hi and remind you about Mary's performance tomorrow. You can still come right?"

"Yes, I would like to, but I have to complete this first. If you want me to go, please leave me alone." Putting his glasses back in place, he turned away from her and continued to work.

She stalked away and ran up the stairs to their bedroom. She knew work stressed him out, but he didn't need to take it out on her. Plopping down on the bed, she looked at all the nice stuff that filled the room. She couldn't complain; she had everything a person could possibly want. *Then why do I feel so empty?*

CHAPTER 10

I think I'm going to throw up. Why did I let him talk me into doing this? I'm going to mess up the song and then God will hate me. I need a good luck lick from Maverick. Mary stepped out the back door and opened the gate. He jumped up and licked her cheek. "Thanks, boy. I needed that."

"Do you always talk to your dog in the dark?"

She jumped and turned around. "Derek? You almost gave me a heart attack."

"Sorry. Who is this handsome guy?"

"Derek, this is Maverick." He bent down and petted the dog's head. Maverick barked in approval and licked his hand. "I think he likes you."

"Lucky for me, since I wouldn't want him to attack me if I tried to kiss you," he teased. "Are you ready to go?"

Her mind became foggy as she imagined him kissing her. *This is absurd; I cannot have these thoughts. He's my friend, and I work with him.* She glanced at him and found his eyes on hers. *It looks like he's waiting for an answer. Did he ask me something? Oh, why does he have to be so cute?*

"Mary, are you okay?"

"What? Yeah, I'm fine. Sorry, I must have spaced out for a second. Are you ready to go?"

Laughing to himself, he followed her to the car. The kiss comment had caught her off guard, like he knew it would. She tried to hide it, but he could tell he had punctured a hole in her wall of ice. It was only a matter of time before the entire thing came down.

Stacey and Clint slipped into the crowded church. It was only quarter to nine, but already adults and children filled the pews. *Everyone must have heard Mary was singing tonight,* she thought as they found a spot near the back. Reaching over, she fixed Clint's collar and gave him a quick peck on the cheek. "I'm glad you could make it."

"Me too. I might have to leave early, but I'm sure Mary can give you a ride home."

"Why? I thought you finished all your work." Her brow burrowed in confusion.

He forced himself to keep his temper even though he wanted to scream at the meddlesome woman who had taken over his fiancé's body. Gritting his teeth, he answered in a harsh whisper. "I did, but there are a few things I need to fix before tomorrow. If this thing runs too late, I'll just duck out early and finish it up."

"Sorry for asking. Leave whenever you want; I know Mary will bring me home."

Trent walked into the church and cringed. Maybe this was a bad idea. He didn't know why he had let that Derek guy talk him into coming; he certainly didn't belong. Just as he was about to make a run for it, Derek spotted him and waved from the front row. *Too late now,* he thought. He put a smile on his lips and politely waved back. He noticed that people filled the pews in almost every row. He couldn't sit near the front even if he wanted to. Thankful for the excuse to sit towards the back, he found an empty seat in the very last row. Before he could change his mind, he forced himself down onto the pew. *At least if it is the same Mary, I'll be able to sneak out before she catches a glimpse of me.*

Only two minutes remained until the service was supposed to start. Mary sat next to Derek in the front row nervously biting her nails and tapping her feet. *Pray. Pray. Pray.* The word seemed to go with the rhythm of her taps. *Help me remember the words to this song. Use my voice to reach the people who are so desperately seeking you. Amen.* At the conclusion of her prayer, she felt the butterflies fly away one by one as God's peace settled over her. She could do this; God was with her.

Pastor Thomas stood in front of the congregation and smiled. "I'd like to welcome all the newcomers tonight. This is usually just a youth service, but tonight we have a special treat for you. The woman who has been working diligently with our high school students has agreed to grace us with her lovely voice. I am pleased to present to you, Mary Canfield." Applause erupted through the audience. "She also requests that instead of clapping at the end of the piece, you remain silent and simply let the words work in your hearts and minds."

Taking a deep breath, Mary rose from the pew and took her place next to the piano. The pianist started out with a soft, flowing melody. Quieting down, the people listened and waited for her voice to join in. She took her cue from the pianist, opened her mouth, and began to sing the Ginny Owens song she had been practicing for so long.

The pathway is broken
And the signs are unclear
And I don't know the reason why you brought me here
But just because you love me the way that you do
I will go through the valley
If you want me to

Now I'm not who I was
When I took my first step
And I'm clinging to the promise
You're not through with me yet
So if all of these trials bring me closer to you
I will go through the fire
If you want me to
It may not be the way I would have chosen
When you lead me through a world that's not my own
But you never said it would be easy
You only said I'll never go alone
So when the whole world turns against me
And I'm all by myself
And I can't hear you answer my cries for help
I'll remember the suffering your love put you through
And I'll go through the valley
If you want me to

Captivated by her voice, the audience sat in awe as she sang the last words. Mary took her seat in the silent room and bowed her head in prayer. Several moments passed before the pastor spoke. "Many of you out there can probably relate to this song. We, as Christians, are tempted everyday with things of the world.

"At some point we all have strayed a little off the path, stumbled over a rock, or have fallen completely on our faces. Our walk with Jesus is far from easy. The important thing is that we pick ourselves up, take Jesus' out-stretched hand, and walk with Him once again.

"Matthew 7:13–14 says, 'You can enter God's kingdom only through the narrow gate. The highway to hell is broad and its gate is wider for the many that choose the easy way. But the gateway to life is small, and the road is narrow, and only a few ever find it.'

"Some of His plans may seem crazy, cruel, or unfair to our human minds, but as His children, we need to be obedient and faithful. As the song says, there will be times that we will be asked to walk through a valley, but we must not give up and choose the easy way. Instead, lean on God for strength and courage with the knowledge that even if every person on earth abandons you, He never will."

Mary's song had opened Stacey's heart enough for the pastor's words to flow right in. *Maybe this is what I've been missing.* She couldn't wait for the service to be over, so she could talk to Mary. So many questions filled her mind as she thought about all the stuff she had just heard. As the congregation stood for the praise and worship songs, she looked over at Clint to see if the words had affected him in any way. A scowl covered his face. "What's the matter?" she whispered.

He blinked. "What? Oh nothing. I was just thinking about all the work I still have to get done, so I should probably head out. Tell Mary she sounded good. I'll see you at home." Avoiding all eye contact and paying no attention to his surroundings, Clint quickly left the pew.

Watching the people around him stand, Trent knew it was the perfect opportunity to leave. He should have known it was going to be her. *Oh well,* he thought, *at least she won't have a chance to see me.* He stepped around people and walked towards the back door. Pulling his hood over his face, he didn't notice the man walking out from the other side of the church. They bumped shoulders slightly and continued on their separate ways without exchanging a single word.

Maria S. Sakry

CHAPTER 11

Derek stood off to the side and searched for Trent after the conclusion of the service. He had seen him just before it had started, but now he was nowhere to be found. *Hmm? Oh well, maybe he just had somewhere he needed to be,* he decided as he turned his gaze to Mary. Watching the people hover around Mary, he smiled with pride as he heard them praise her for her singing and her work with the students. They certainly loved her, and he could understand why. He noticed how her cheeks turned red at each compliment, and how her humble nature allowed her only to give credit to God for what He accomplished through her. Derek had never met anyone quite like her.

"An admiring fan?" the woman next to him inquired.

Derek laughed. "I guess you could say that. I actually work with Mary down at the station, and she invited me here tonight."

"Ah, you must be Derek."

Do I know this woman? Confused, he stared at her, but there was no spark of recognition. "I'm sorry, have we met before."

It was her turn to laugh. "No, I'm sorry. I didn't mean to freak you out. My name is Stacey Hartman, and I am Mary's best friend. She's talked about you." She gave him a wink and glanced at Mary. "She's an incredible person who has been through a lot, so if you break her heart, I'll have to hurt you. Okay?"

"Okay, but I don't understand. We're just friends, so how could I break her heart?"

"Men are so dense," she sighed dramatically, then continued. "She wouldn't have invited you tonight if she didn't like you. Normally she stays far way from young, attractive men such as yourself, so obviously something has changed."

"So, you mean she—"

"Hey, you two, I'm sorry about all that," Mary cut in.

"Don't be. You have a beautiful gift, and you used it tonight to reach people." Stacey wrapped her arms around her and gave her a quick hug. "You even reached me."

Mary broke away and looked at her best friend. "Really? I did?"

She nodded and a wide grin spread across her face. "I still have a lot of questions for you before I decide anything for sure. Is it all right if I badger you on the way home? Clint had to leave early, so I was wondering if I could get a ride from you."

"Well, Derek drove me here," Mary explained. Stacey caught his eye and smirked. "Oh, how rude of me, I forgot to introduce you two."

"It's okay we met a few minutes ago, and it would be my pleasure to escort you lovely women home." He offered them each an arm and gave Mary a smile. *She likes me. Lord, help me be the man she needs me to be. I want to take care of her.*

"John 3:16–18 states, 'For God so loved the world that he gave his only Son, so that everyone that believes in him will not perish but have eternal life. God did not send his Son into the world to condemn it, but to save it. There is no judgment awaiting those who trust him. But those who do not trust him have already been judged for not believing in the only Son of God.' So you see, whatever sin you have committed can be forgiven if you open your heart to Jesus and believe in Him. Christ died so that we could be forgiven. He alone bridges the gap between man and God; He is the only way to heaven."

Stacey stood in the foyer of her house and stared at Mary. All the things she said made complete sense, especially after hearing the song and the pastor's sermon. She wanted what Mary had. She wanted the peace that came with becoming a Christian. The emptiness she felt needed to be filled with the only thing that could fill it—Jesus. The only problem was that she didn't know if she was ready. "Mary, what if I make this decision, but then I realize I can't keep going. What if I revert back to my old ways?" She looked at her hands and sighed. "I just don't want to disappoint anyone."

Mary stepped over and gently took her hands. "It is a very important decision, and it's one that should not be taken lightly, but I strongly urge you not to wait. If you know right now that you want Jesus in your heart and in your life, ask him. Asking him is the way to salvation. Romans 10:9–10 says, 'For if you confess with your mouth that Jesus is Lord and believe in your heart that God raised him from the dead, you will be saved. For it is by believing in your heart that you are made right with God, and it is by confessing with your mouth that you are saved.'

"Tell him, Stace, that you believe in Him and want Him at the center of your life, and don't worry about messing up. If you do make a mistake, don't let yourself turn back to your old ways. Ask God for strength, and He will help you overcome any obstacle. I will also be here for you if you ever need anything or have any questions. There is also the church, Pastor Thomas, and the people there to help you too. It is your decision, but if you can hear God speaking to your heart, don't wait. He wants you, and He loves you very much."

Stacey's eyes filled with tears as she mulled over Mary's words. *Do you want me God?* She silently prayed. *"I stand outside the entrance of your heart and knock. Will you let me in?"* The words uncontrollably popped into her thoughts as if someone were speaking to her. The tears flowed harder and her lips trembled as she fell to her knees and prayed aloud. "Yes, I'll let you in. I want you in my life, and I am so sorry for my past and not believing in you. I love you, Jesus. Please forgive me."

Mary knelt beside her and gently stroked her back. "You did it, Stace." Her friend sat up and looked at her through moist eyes. "I am so proud of you. I love you." She pulled Stacey close and held her tight. "You're my best friend, and I couldn't imagine heaven without you in it."

Stacey hugged her back. "Thank you, Mary, for everything. I don't know what I would do without you." She let out a small laugh. "I guess this means I'll have to dust off the old Bible and start going to church with you. I mean, if that's okay."

"Of course it is. I would love for you to come with me. I have a word of advice on the Bible, though—start in the New Testament at Matthew and work your way through. It'll make more sense that way, but if something does come up that confuses you, don't hesitate to call. I love you." She gave her another squeeze and let go. "I guess I should get back out there before Derek leaves me here."

Stacey laughed and wiped away the tears. "I don't think that man would leave you anywhere."

Mary gawked at her. "What do you mean by that? We're just friends. He doesn't think of me in that way, and I don't think of him like that. Even if he is the cutest man I've ever met and likes to help people, I don't care. He is just my friend."

"Are you trying to convince me or yourself of that fact? Look Mary, it's okay if you have feelings for the guy. You of all people deserve to have a great man like that interested in you. Don't ruin it. Don't push him away like you have so many others. I know you're scared and uncertain about what is going to happen with all the stalker stuff, but I'm sure Derek would be more than willing to help you through it. Let him in, Mary. Let him in."

Mary nodded her head and blinked her eyelids rapidly to prevent the tears from falling. "I know you're right. It's just so hard right now. I didn't want to like him. I didn't want him in my life. He's just so incredible; I can't help it. It's just that my future is so uncertain, and I don't want to hurt him."

"I'm not saying you need to marry the guy right now. Just tell him about your situation and explain to him what has been going on. If he really cares about you like I know he does, then he will find a way to help you. Then maybe your future will become clearer." Stacey gave her a quick hug. "Thanks for helping me with my decision tonight, and don't worry—everything will work out just fine. I'll talk to you later. Now get going."

"Yes mother," she smiled meekly. "I'll see you later, my dear sister in Christ."

Sister in Christ, she liked the sound of that. Stacey

watched Mary walk to the car and sighed. Deep down she was really worried about her. She didn't want to lose her best friend. *Pray.* The word came to her. *Well, I don't know if I'm doing this right since I just became a Christian, but God, please be with Mary during this difficult time and keep her safe. I need her. Amen.*

Derek's gaze never left Mary's shadowed figure as it moved back towards his car. Stacey's words played over and over in his head. *Mary's been through a lot. Don't break her heart.* He wondered what she had been through. He liked her a lot, but he felt like he was left out of a major part of her life. As she climbed into the car, he noticed she had been crying. Instinctively he reached over and lightly brushed his fingertips across her cheek where traces of the tears still remained. "Are you okay?"

"Yes, I am more than okay. Stacey just became a Christian."

"Well, that's wonderful!" he exclaimed and gave her a huge grin.

She smiled in return as she filled him in on every detail of the miracle she had just been a part of. "I'm so happy for her. I've been praying for her for so long. I am incredibly thankful that God finally reached her and allowed me to be a part of it."

"Yes, we do serve a wonderful Lord," he answered as he searched her eyes with his own. Something wasn't right. He studied them closely until he realized what it was. The sparkle that usually danced around her eyes when she smiled had been replaced with a deep sadness. "Mary, what is wrong?"

She looked away and took a deep breath. "There are

a lot of things wrong. Things that I want to tell you, but I'm not quite ready yet because it's complicated. I never planned on meeting anyone, especially at this point in my life. I really like you, Derek, but there are some things happening right now that I don't want to drag you into." An exasperated sigh escaped her lips. "I'm sorry. I'm sure that made absolutely no sense."

He lifted up her chin slightly and looked deep into her sapphire eyes. "I understand completely. I like you a lot too, and I'll be here whenever you're ready to talk." He lowered his head and softly kissed her forehead. "I want to help you."

"Thanks, Derek, it really means a lot to me." She turned towards the window and tried to ignore how close his lips had been. *How could one pair of lips be so distracting and so intense?* The spot on her forehead still tingled from his kiss.

Derek put the car into drive and followed the road to Mary's house. As he drove, his thoughts were filled with kissing her. It had been a struggle to pull his eyes away from hers and kiss her forehead instead of kissing her perfect mouth. *Get a grip, man.* He needed to take things slow. He pulled into the driveway and parked the car. "Can I walk you to your door?"

Mary stared up at the front porch and blinked her eyes to make sure what she saw was real. The dull porch light made it harder for her to see, but she could make out an object on the wooden panels. Forcing herself to remain calm, she answered slowly. "No, it's okay. It's kind of late. I can just let myself in."

Not waiting for a response, she hopped out of the car and walked briskly up to the house. *What is it? I'm pretty sure I didn't leave anything out here,* she thought as she climbed up the porch steps. Her eyes fell on the object. *My pants.* Gasping for air, she grabbed onto the railing. *How could he do this? How could he bring those back here after all this time?* She felt sick to her stomach. *I need to lie down.* She tried to walk to the door, but the porch started to spin. Unable to make it stop, the darkness overtook her as she slipped into unconsciousness.

Derek caught Mary just as she was about to hit the cold, hard porch. He had been waiting in his car for her to get into the house when her face had turned as white as the snow. Knowing something was wrong; he had jumped out immediately to help her. Now he held her close and looked around to figure out what had scared her so badly. *All I see is a ripped pair of pants.* He couldn't understand how something like that could make a person faint, but the only way he was going to find out was to have Mary tell him.

He dug into her coat pocket for the house keys. Finding them quickly, he opened the door and brought her inside to the couch. Her face remained pale as he took off the coat and covered her with blankets. "Mary, can you hear me? Wake up if you can hear me." He rubbed her arms and continued to speak quietly to her.

She slowly woke up and groggily looked at Derek. "What happened? What are you doing in here?"

"Mary, you fainted. I'm not sure why, but I was hoping you could tell me."

Her eyes widened and her breath quickened as she thought about those pants.

Derek noticed her anxiety and gently took her hand.

"It's okay, Mary. I'm here now. Nothing is going to happen to you. I'm here. I will protect you."

She reached out to him and wrapped her arms around his broad shoulders. Hugging him tightly, she began to cry. "I'm so scared, Derek. Thank you for being here. She sniffed softy and looked up at him. "Can you call Detective Benson for me? His card is hanging up on the refrigerator. He needs to know about this, and I don't think I can handle talking on the phone."

"Of course I can. If there is anything you need me to do, just ask." He hugged her for another minute before getting up to get the phone and the number. He never wanted to let go of her. He wanted to help her and help make the fear go away. He didn't want to pry, but he wanted to know what was going on. His curiosity was driving him crazy. Running his fingers through his hair, he let out a deep breath and dialed the number.

"Detective Benson, this is Derek Elstrom. I'm a friend of Mary Canfield. There's been sort of a situation here tonight, and she wants you to come and check it out if you can." He waited for the detective's reply. "Okay, sounds good, thank you, sir."

"What did he say? Will he come here?" Mary asked nervously.

"He said he had something to finish up quick, and then he'd come right over. Do you want me to stay with you until he gets here?"

"Yes, I would like that very much. Could you bring Maverick in too?"

Staring into her pleading eyes, he nodded his head. "Of course, I would do anything for you." He shook his head as he walked to the back door. He had it bad for this woman. Actually it was more than that. He felt more for her than he had ever felt for any other woman. He stopped dead in his tracks, his thoughts cementing him to the floor. *Oh my goodness, I'm in love with Mary.*

Maria S. Sakry

CHAPTER 12

It amazed him how stupid people could be. First, he had been invited to watch Mary sing, and then that clumsy fool had bumped into him. That man was lucky he hadn't wanted to draw any attention to himself, or he would have made him pay for his inept actions.

He shook his head and smirked. He couldn't believe he had sat there without anyone knowing his true identity. His smirk turned to a sneer as he thought about the stupid girl. Hearing her sing about God's love had almost been his undoing. It had taken every ounce of self-control not to jump the pews and strangle her. He was thankful that he had been able to slip out early enough to leave a little surprise for her. He wished he could have stayed to see her face when she found it, but he couldn't take any more chances tonight. Besides, he knew there would be plenty of other opportunities to watch her shake with fear.

Moving his clothes aside, he stared at the most recent picture of her and traced the outline of her lips with his index finger. Oh, how he longed to touch her again and run his hands all over that smooth skin. *Soon*, he thought, *very soon I will be able to do whatever I want to you. Sleep well, Mary, if you can.* He pushed the clothes back in place and walked into his bedroom.

"Come here, honey. What took you so long?" the woman in his bed called to him.

"I was just taking care of some last-minute business, but I'm here now," he replied as he lay down next to her.

She turned towards him and gave him a deep kiss. "Well, I'm glad you are. I missed you."

He continued to kiss her, but in his mind, he was kissing Mary. He pictured her being here with him, laughing with him, and loving him. They could have been so happy together, but she had ruined it. This time she didn't have a choice. After he got done with her, she would belong to him forever.

CHAPTER 13

Yawning loudly and stretching out his back, Trent sat on his king-sized bed and sniffed the air. Aromas of fresh coffee and muffins floated past his nose. He smiled and left the room. Walking towards the kitchen, he realized he could get very used to having someone around. He found Kim washing the dishes while food cooled on the counter.

"Well, good morning. Thanks for making breakfast. You're spoiling me, you know," he told her as he came up behind her and planted a kiss on her lips.

"I know, but I enjoy cooking for you. I have to leave for work, but can I see you tonight?" she asked with a flutter of her eyelashes.

"Sure, sounds good to me." He went in for another kiss before she left. "I'll see you later."

"Bye, honey."

He looked after her as she walked to her car. He cringed when he thought about her calling him honey. They had only known each other a few days, but she was acting like they had been together forever. He liked her a lot, but he wasn't looking for anything really serious, just someone to spend time with and keep him distracted. Mary's voice still haunted him from the night before. He never knew she could sing like that. He couldn't get her out of his head. *That problem should be resolved though in a few weeks when I go see her,* he thought as he threw on a pair of jeans and a t-shirt and headed out the door.

Derek punched the bag violently with a right hook, then a left. The black punching bag swung back and forth as he took his frustration out on it. How could one woman be so irresistible, yet so infuriating at the same time? Last night he found out he was in love with the woman who refused to tell him anything. She faints, and he's supposed to ignore it like it's nothing at all.

He gave the bag another punch. *Why can't she just tell me what's going on?* It didn't help him find anything out either when she had asked him to leave as soon as the detective showed up. All he had overheard was the word rape. *Rape.* That word alone made him hit the bag three times successively. *Lord, I know she is going through a hard time, but please help her open up to me. I don't want to intrude into her life, but I am really worried about her.* He took two more swings and sat down for a water break.

"Dude, you really need to calm down. What did that bag ever do to you?" Eric slapped him on the back. "You're a vicious animal today. Is something up?"

Stretching out his arms, he sighed and looked over at his friend. "Yeah, I'm having some girl trouble." Noticing the amused gleam in Eric's eye, he continued. "It's not what you're thinking. Mary, my partner at the station, is in some kind of trouble, but she won't tell me what it is. I'm really worried about her. I want to keep her safe."

"Your *partner?*" Eric scoffed as he took in his friend's attitude and body language. "It's more than that. You've fallen in love with her, haven't you?"

"What? How…? How could you even know that? I just figured out I had last night," he explained as he gave him a friendly punch in the arm.

"Watch it, man. Don't make me kick your butt." He

grinned at him. "It's not my fault your feelings are written all over your face."

"I know, but it's crazy that I'm feeling this way. I've only known her for a few days. Love can't happen that fast, can it?"

"I think when it comes to love, anything is possible." Eric realized what he had just said and hooted with laughter. "Wow, that was corny. Please erase all memory of that statement."

Derek laughed with him. "I will—don't worry. But I think you're right. I do love her, so I guess I have to be patient and wait for her to come to me. There is just one problem though—I hate being patient."

"Well, some one-on-one might help pass the time if you think you stand a chance at beating me." He tossed the basketball at him. "Let's play."

He grabbed the ball out of the air. "I guess I haven't beaten you in awhile, so this will definitely make me feel better." Thankful Eric had come in when he did; he dribbled the ball past him and headed for the basket. Playing him would be a good distraction. Although when it came to Mary, he knew he could wait forever if he had to.

Monday morning, Detective Benson paced the carpeted floor of his office. The Canfield situation bothered him greatly. The pair of pants that had been left on her porch last night had gotten him nowhere. Not a single substance could be found on them. Whoever had left those and the notes obviously knew what they were doing. It frustrated him beyond words that no leads had turned up. It also didn't help that they couldn't waste any more time on a stalking case until some real evidence showed up. He needed a fingerprint, a piece of hair—something—but none had surfaced. They didn't even have a single suspect. It could be the man that raped her, whoever that was. Then again, anyone could have been stalking Mary, found out what happened to her, and tried to make her suffer over and over again. Even the pants weren't necessarily hers; they could just be an identical pair to the ones she had lost that night.

Huffing loudly, he plopped down into his chair and rested his balding head in his hands. He wanted to help, but the police force just didn't have enough manpower to have someone sit and constantly watch her house, especially if nothing happened for the third consecutive year. But what if something did, and they were too late? The question had been plaguing him all night, and in the morning light, he wasn't any closer to finding an answer. Knowing he had other cases that needed his time and attention, he pushed the thoughts of Mary, stalkers, and rape from his mind and opened a file at the top of his stack. Before settling in to read, he bowed his head and whispered softly, "Please keep her safe."

Mary forgot all her troubles and fears as she focused on the emergency at hand. A car accident had just been called in. With its lights flashing and sirens blaring, ambulance nine moved quickly through the traffic. Matt drove while Mary navigated to the intersection of Fourth Street and Pine. Anticipating the seriousness of the accident, her heart raced. She loved her job, and she did it well; sometimes, though, her nerves got the best of her. She prayed silently for God to give her courage, strength, and wisdom as they neared the scene. Nervousness gave way to determination by the time they parked behind the smashed-up car.

She saw a large delivery truck, a car, and the first responders already on the scene. One of the first responders stood with the driver of the truck. Speaking loudly and wildly waving his hands, the driver seemed angry but unharmed. Knowing he was in good hands, she walked hurriedly over to the damaged vehicle. The driver's side of the car had suffered very little compared to the passenger side. They had already gotten the driver out, a middle-aged mom with only a few bruises. Her son, however, remained in the backseat. Unable to open the back passenger door since the truck had hit hard on the right rear side, they had to get him out another way.

"What is his name?" Mary asked his mother as she surveyed the car.

"Cody," the mother answered breathlessly. "Is he going to be okay?"

"I don't know, but we are going to do our best to help him." Taking a deep breath, she peered in through the left back car door. The impact of the accident had caused his head to flop to the left, making the right side of his head clearly visible. She noticed the skull had been crushed and a massive wound bled profusely. She spoke gently but urgently to the young boy. "Cody, can you hear me?" He did not respond. Rubbing his sternum firmly, she observed him to see if he would make any movement. Again there was nothing. She looked over at Larry, the other first responder that held Cody's neck in place. "We need to get him out of here." Larry nodded in affirmation.

He continued to hold his neck while Mary applied a cervical collar. Once the collar was in place, Larry continued to hold it while Mary quickly examined Cody. Keeping her emotions in check, she bandaged the gushing wound and taped some padding around the head. Moving through her examination, she thought the right side of his abdomen seemed a bit distended. Knowing that he may have a floating rib, she expertly padded the area and bandaged that up as well. She didn't notice anything else that needed immediate attention as she quickly scanned the rest of the body. Nodding to Matt, he helped her maneuver the child out of the car and towards the backboard and stretcher. Careful not to bump the oxygen mask out of place, they successfully got him out.

While she finished securing Cody onto the backboard with Larry's help, Matt situated the mother in the back of the ambulance and checked her vital signs. Since the mother's vital signs fell within a normal range, Matt hopped out of the back of the ambulance and helped Mary load the patient into the ambulance. "I think we're all set," he told her. "Why don't you stay with the patient, and I'll drive?"

"Okay," she agreed and climbed into the back. Matt shut the doors behind her and jumped into the driver's seat. While he drove hurriedly, but safely to the hospital, she checked Cody's vitals. She hoped and prayed that they made it in time, but the situation didn't look good. The mother sat behind her and wept for her child. Mary sat down next to her and reached for her wrist. "I just want to get a set of vitals to make sure you're doing okay," Mary explained as her fingertips touched the woman's skin.

"Don't touch me!" the woman snapped and pulled her hand away. "Your partner just did that. I am fine, just save him." The woman began to sob loudly. "He has to live. He's all I have."

Before Mary could respond, the ambulance stopped. Matt swung the back doors open, and they rolled the stretcher out and into the ER. The mother clung tightly to the metal rail of the stretcher and walked with them. As soon as they got inside, two nurses took over and rolled him immediately into the operating room while another nurse stayed with the mother.

Matt and Mary waited around until one of the nurses came over with a clipboard to get the patients' information. Her face looked grim. Mary felt a sinking feeling in her stomach. A part of her knew he hadn't made it. The mother proved Mary's intuition when she broke down, her wailing filling the room. The thought of losing a child pierced Mary's heart, but she couldn't let her feelings show. As a paramedic, she knew there were some patients she just couldn't save; it didn't matter how hard she tried. She dealt with the pain of her losses in private, never on the job.

She turned to leave and walked with Matt towards the exit. Before she could get out the door, she felt herself being pulled from behind. The mother of the child spun her around by her coat and started hitting her. "You killed him! It's all your fault! Why weren't you there sooner?" she screamed at the top of her lungs. Instinctively, Mary raised her arms to try and block the mother's swinging fists.

"What are you doing?" Matt yelled as he rushed in and pulled the woman off of Mary. All the yelling and crying finally took its toll on the poor woman. She collapsed in his arms just as two nurses rushed over. Taking her from him, they apologized for the outburst and brought her to a room.

Matt turned to Mary. "Are you okay?" He could see a red mark on her cheek that he figured would bruise, but other than that, the woman had mainly hit her arms. "Mary? Answer me. Are you okay?"

Mary stood completely still, even her brain refused to function. She couldn't hear anything or see anyone around her. It seemed as if she had entered a black room. She couldn't even feel the hands that caught her when her legs gave out. Oblivious to the world, her body and mind relaxed into a strange, dark place.

A few moments later, Mary awoke on a stretcher and found Matt's worried eyes staring at her. "Why am I on this thing? Get me down."

"No, you need to just sit for a few moments. You just went into complete shock after that woman attacked you, and you passed out. Your reaction is understandable, and you're not in any trouble, so don't worry. I called the station and told them what happened. We're out of the rotation for the next half hour, so you can take a minute to breathe. Okay?" he explained firmly.

"Okay, dad," she joked and gave him a small smile. "I'm sorry."

Giving her a serious look, the older man began to speak. "You *know* you've become like a daughter to me. When Pam and I found out we could never have children, it hurt a lot. We would have made great parents, but God had other plans. To tell you the truth, though, I didn't know what His plans were until you walked into the station that first day. I saw you and wanted to take you under my wing right away. I figured you would need a lot of help and someone to show you the ropes. You surprised me, though, with your spunk, smarts, and love for the job. You handled the first calls you ran with me like a pro. I thought I would be the one to teach you all I knew, but you ended up teaching me some things too. You allowed me to be a part of your life. I do know that I will never have a daughter of my own, but I also know that if did, I would have wanted her to be just like you."

He paused slightly then continued. "I'm telling you all of this because I want you to understand that no part of today was your fault. You did everything right, and I am so proud of you. That mother simply took her anger and guilt out on you. You see, she was the one at fault. She ran the light and killed her son."

Mary felt her eyes begin to well up as she threw her arms around him. "Oh my goodness! No wonder she reacted the way she did—she just couldn't bear all that pain. I wish I could have done more. I wanted to save him so badly. I'm glad you're still proud of me. I've often thought of you as a second dad." She gave him a tight squeeze and then broke the embrace. "Thank you for the talk. I really needed it. I guess I'm ready to get back out there."

"Well, I am glad to hear that, but you're done for the day. You know the rules. If anything happens to you on the job, including fainting, you get sent home. We'll head back to the station, so I can drop you off and pick up Kent."

"Fine. I guess I don't have a choice." Replying glumly, she jumped down and stood beside Matt.

"Oh, and one more thing, you might want to put some

ice on that nice shiner of yours. It's going to be a beauty. You should be proud," he teased.

She could feel the throbbing on her left cheek and up under her eye. *Great*, she thought, *just what I didn't need.* "Oh, I am. I've always wanted a black eye."

CHAPTER 14

A few hours later, Mary sat on her front porch and reflected on the day. Images of the crushed skull she had seen uncontrollably popped into her head. Shuddering, she pushed them from her thoughts. Maverick looked over at her and placed his head upon her shoulder. She leaned over and rested her head on top of his. "It's been a rough day, boy." She still wished she could have magically made that little boy live. Sighing loudly, she replayed the accident scene over and over again, searching for any mistakes in her care. She hadn't made any. Matt's words came back to her and brought with them a deep peace. She had done her best, and he was proud of her.

Mary stood up and stretched out her long legs. "How does a run sound, Mav?" Maverick barked in agreement. Mary ran inside quick to grab his leash when the phone rang. "Hello," she answered.

"Mary? Is that you? Are you okay?"

"Yes, Sandra, it's me." She replied when she recognized her older sister's voice. "I'm fine."

"You sound out of breath."

"Oh, really, well, I just ran up the steps quick to grab Maverick's leash, so we could go for a run. I must be out of shape. I guess you haven't seen me in a month. I probably have gotten really fat since then."

"Ha! Yeah right, miss toothpick. Anyways, I was just calling to see how you were doing. We haven't talked in over a week. I've been kind of busy, but you haven't even tried to call me. What's the deal?"

"Ah, I've just been busy with work and stuff. I'm sorry."

"No, that's not it. Is something wrong? You know you can't keep secrets from me. What happened?"

Mary huffed loudly in the phone. Her sister could be so exasperating. How could she always know when she was keeping something from her? She found it quite annoying. Not wanting to bring up the letters yet, she thought of something else. "Well, I guess something did sort of happen," she began. Mary filled her in about the car accident and the little boy dying. Then she finished off with the mom giving her a black eye and fainting in the hospital.

"Oh my goodness, are you okay now? Should I come down there? A black eye! Is it going to be gone before the wedding next week? A little boy died? Was it your fault? What am I saying—of course it wasn't your fault!" Sandra fired the words out of her mouth like an AK-47 firing out bullets.

Thankful that Sandra had fallen for the decoy, Mary almost had to laugh at her sister's worries. "Whoa! Slow down, turbo! I am fine. It hurt a lot to lose a patient, but I know I did everything in my power to save him. The black eye will hopefully be gone by next Saturday, or Grace will have some very colorful wedding pictures. I am okay now, so you don't need to come down here. I'll see you this weekend when we take Grace out dancing, and I will be home next Friday for the rehearsal dinner. Speaking of which, what are you going to wear? Are we supposed to dress up for the dinner?"

"I'll probably wear my little black dress with a pair of

strappy heels. What about you? Actually, a more important question is who are you going to bring?"

"Ah, I'm not sure about what I'm wearing yet, and I didn't think we had to bring anyone."

"Mary, you'll be the only one there without a date. You told me over a month ago when we talked about this that you would bring someone. I knew this was going to happen. Thank goodness I planned for it."

"What? What do you mean by that?" Mary questioned.

"Well, I just knew you wouldn't find anyone. I mean, come on. You haven't been on a date in over three years. It probably doesn't help that you completely ignore any man that so much as looks in your direction. I figured you might need a little bit of help, so I found someone."

"What do you mean you found someone? Was it some random person off the street or what?"

Sandra giggled loudly. "No, silly, I wouldn't do that to you. It's one of Ryan's friends, Jack. He comes over all the time to play cards and darts with us. Every time he's over, he stares at your picture for at least five minutes and asks if you're still single."

"Ha! He does not. You're so full of it."

"No, I'm serious. He's a great guy, very good looking, tall, smart, funny, and he goes to church."

"Well, why don't you date him then?"

"Mary! Why aren't you happy about this? I just did you a huge favor. Now you don't have to spend the weekend alone. You'll have someone to dance with and talk to."

Mary remained silent. Why couldn't her family understand that she liked being there to spend time with them?

She was happy with her life. She didn't need anyone special like they did. Derek's face floated through her thoughts. She angrily pushed it away and continued to pout.

"Look, Mar," Sandra began again in a softer voice. "I just want you to be happy. We all do. I know you've been through some tough things, but at some point you just need to let it go. The letters have stopped, right? There is nothing holding you back now. Don't worry about the past. It's done now. He can't hurt you anymore."

Mary took a few deep breaths and tried not to cry. Her sister would understand if she just knew the truth, but she couldn't tell her. She didn't have the heart to ruin her younger sister's special day. She knew that would happen if she told Sandra everything. She would then tell their parents, and everyone would soon know. Everyone would worry just like the other years. They didn't need that again. They all needed to move on and be happy. This year, she decided, she had to keep it to herself. "Yes, Sandra, you're right. I do appreciate the effort, but I just feel weird spending the weekend with someone I hardly know. I have a friend I think I could bring...it's a guy. Would that be acceptable?"

"You do? What guy? All your guy friends are married or as old as dad. Don't tell me you're bringing one of them."

Mary had to laugh. "No, it's this new guy that started at the station last week. His name is Derek, and he's very nice. I'll bring him."

"Well, good. Jack will be very disappointed, though. Have you gotten the speech written yet, Miss Maid of Honor?"

"Not quite. I have the notebook ready though."

"You haven't even started it yet?" she asked incredulously.

"Do you mean technically?"

"Mary! It's like a week away. You better get a move on it. Oh, my dinner is burning. I guess I should let you go. I'll see you this weekend, though. I want to hear all about this mysterious Derek guy. Love you."

"Love you too. Bye." Mary shook her head at her crazy sister. She had really missed her. Actually she missed her whole family. She couldn't wait to go home next weekend and see everyone. Remembering the date situation, she closed her eyes. *Derek.* Why did she say she could bring him? She couldn't even face him right now because of last night. He probably thought she was completely crazy, and a black eye certainly didn't help her case. How in the world could she ask him to her sister's wedding?

Derek stepped out of his car and glanced over the bushes that separated Eric's yard from Mary's. He noticed Maverick sitting all alone on the front steps and decided to go over to investigate the situation. As he climbed through the bushes, Maverick spotted him and yipped playfully. "Hey, boy, how are you?" He asked as he rubbed behind the Great Dane's ears. "Where's Mary at?" Maverick barked and looked towards the house. "Thanks."

He knocked loudly and listened for a reply but none came. Scared that something had happened, he opened the door and called her name as he entered the kitchen. When he found her, his feet came to an abrupt halt. She sat weeping at the table with a picture in her hand. "Mary," he softly whispered her name. "Are you okay?"

She slowly shook her head no and continued to cry.

He stepped behind her and gently placed his hands on her shoulders. "I'm here for you, Mary. Why don't you let me in? Why can't you tell me what is wrong? Trust me. Please trust me, Mary. I want to help you." He watched as she raised her head and looked into his eyes. Gasping when he saw the black-and-blue mark on her face, he stumbled backwards. "Who did this to you?" He felt sick with rage. *How could anyone damage such soft, perfect skin? How could anyone harm such a gentle, loving woman?*

"It's a long story, and it's been a really long day," she protested.

"Well, lucky for you, I have all the time in the world. I just have to run over to Eric's quick and tell him that I can't play NBA Live tonight. He'll understand, so don't worry. Then I will come back here, cook for you, and you can tell me all about it. How does that sound?"

"Good, I guess."

"Great! While I'm over there think about whether you prefer Dominos or Pizza Hut better." Giving her a wink, he left the house and headed over to Eric's.

Mary had to laugh at his unusual way of cheering her up. Somehow it worked. She felt so foolish that he had found her crying. She hadn't wanted to cry, but after talking to her sister and thinking about her family, she just broke down. Looking at the picture from Sandra's wedding two years earlier had made her realize how much she missed spending time with her family and telling them about her problems. Holding everything in for so long had finally caused her to crack, but now there were even more things to explain to Derek.

"Derek," she spoke quietly. She smiled at the way his name rolled so smoothly off her tongue. She liked him a lot, and she could tell he liked her too. Knowing that terrified her—she knew her secrets could hurt him and make him turn away. *Help me tell him, Lord, and please help him understand. Please...*

The door swung open in the middle of her prayer and Maverick came bounding in followed by Derek. "Hey, he looked a little lonely out front, so I thought I'd bring him in. Did you decide what you wanted me to make?"

She let out a laugh. "Dominos sounds wonderful."

"Hand me the phone and I'll get cooking."

Once the ordering was done and Maverick had been put in the backyard with his own food, Derek joined Mary on the couch. "Now, how about you tell me about what happened today while we wait for the food to arrive."

"Okay," she agreed and told him about her day.

When she finished, he reached over and held her close for a few moments. "I am so sorry you lost him. You know you did your best, right? That mother had no right to accuse you or hit you."

"I know. I'm okay now. It was just a hard day on top of a hard couple of weeks. Then my sister called this afternoon and badgered me about bringing a date to my younger sister's wedding next weekend. During our conversation, she ended up bringing up some stuff that happened a few years ago and pretty much told me I needed to start dating again. I agreed with her just so she wouldn't pry anymore into my life, and then she tells me she knows the perfect man to be my date. I freak out because I don't even know this person and end up telling her that I'm bringing you. Then after I hang up with her, I start to cry because I hate keeping things from my sister, I miss my family like crazy, and I am so tired of holding everything in."

"Wow, you do have a lot going on. I want to help, Mary. I want you to tell me about last night and what's been happening. Holding all that stuff in is not good for you. Besides, I won't go to your sister's wedding unless you tell me everything."

"Oh, blackmail, huh? Fine, but you have to promise you'll still go with me even if you hate me after I tell you all this stuff."

"I could never hate you, Mary, and there is nothing you could tell me that would keep me from going with you next weekend."

Staring deep into his kind, blue eyes, she knew it was finally time to tell him. "Derek, almost three years ago, I was raped."

CHAPTER 15

The cool breeze blew past Stacey and flipped the pages in her Bible. Sitting alone on her balcony in the fresh air, she stared up at the stars and marveled at their beauty. Some sparkled brightly while others only had a soft glow about them. Together, they created a wondrous masterpiece. Shivering in her gray, knit sweater, she snuggled further under the warm quilt and closed the book.

Tears began to work their way down her cheeks as she thought about the passages she had just read. She couldn't believe how much Jesus had suffered for all of mankind. It broke her heart to think about how long she had rejected him when he had done so much for her. She bowed her head and thanked God again for showing her the way. Looking up once again at the sky, her thoughts turned to Mary. For some reason she felt an undeniable urge to pray for her. In a voice barely above a whisper, she began to speak. "Lord, I am still new at this, but please help her. I don't know if she is in trouble right now or just needs a prayer, but please help her wherever she may be. Keep her safe and give her wisdom and strength. Amen."

"What in the world are you doing out here? Have you completely lost your mind?"

Gasping, Stacey spun around in her chair. "Oh my goodness, Clint, I was praying. You scared me half to death. Didn't your mother ever tell you not to sneak up on people?" she teased and gave him a loving smile.

He returned her smile with a sneer. "Actually, she

didn't. She died when I was seven, remember, and even when she lived, she was a complete waste of a human being," he scoffed bitterly.

Her face paled. How could she have forgotten? She remembered now that he had mentioned his mother's passing, but her words had been innocent enough. She hadn't meant to hurt him. She couldn't have known that his mom was not a good mother since he refused to speak about his family. She guiltily arose from the rocking chair and stepped towards him. "Oh, honey, I am so sorry."

Noticing Stacey's frightened expression, Clint relaxed and let his fiancé's arms envelope him in a hug. He softly kissed her forehead. "It's okay, Stace. I'm sorry for overreacting. I love you. Do you forgive me?"

"Of course I do."

"Praying, huh? Since when have you been into God?" he asked nicely.

"Well, since we went to church. I didn't know how you would take the news, so I wanted to tell you at the right moment." She looked into his eyes. "I became a Christian yesterday."

"Really? Wow, Stace, that's really great. I'm so happy for you." He gave her forehead another kiss.

"You're not mad? I mean, you seemed kind of unhappy yesterday at church."

"No, yesterday I just had a lot on my mind. My thoughts weren't even on God. I'm happy for you, really."

"I'm so glad." She gave him a big smile. "I love you." She pulled him closer and closed her eyes. She wished they could have more of these moments instead of his frequent moments of anger. Lately he had been so edgy with her, and she didn't know why. She knew he had a lot going on at work, but she wished he'd share his problems with her instead of getting upset. Refusing to let her qualms ruin this time with him, she pushed his moody episodes from her mind and drank in the delicious scent of his cologne. She couldn't help but smile to herself as she held the man she knew she would love forever.

Hoping to block a full-blown headache, Mary squeezed her eyes shut and tried to will the pain away. Her mind had completely blanked at Derek's reaction to her first statement. When he had pulled her close and softly whispered in her ear, she had melted. His throat thick with tears, he softly told her how deeply sorry he was and that it wasn't her fault. His tenderness had turned her brain to mush. Now all she wanted to do was cry in his arms. *I need help!* she pleaded. *"I am here,"* she heard a voice speak to her heart. *I can't tell him. Please help me, Lord.* Remaining silent, she listened and heard it again: *"I am here."*

Knowing God was with her, she stubbornly pushed the urge to cry away and broke their hug. "This is the hardest thing for me to talk about, so I need to start talking before I start to cry." He reached over and gently rubbed the back of her hand as she continued. "It happened on April 7, my sophomore year of college." The words brought her back to that dark, lonely night.

The last of the customers finally left as Mary closed her cash register at Amber's, the local department store. Trying hard to hold the tears back, she counted the correct amount to leave in the drawer. She couldn't believe the engine in her car had died. Her dad had called on her break to tell her the bad news; ever since, she had felt weighed down with worry. How could she afford a new car or a new engine? Right now, she had her dad's car, but he would need it back soon. What was she going to do?

As soon as she finished up, she grabbed her things and headed out the door. Hitting her lightly on the face, the fresh air called to her. *I need a walk*, she thought to herself. *Just a quick one down by the lake.* Lately, she had been going there a lot to clear her head. All the stress in her life seemed to suffocate her more and more with each passing day. With homework and bills piling up, issues with friends and work—and now her car—it just got to be too much.

Making up her mind to go, she unlocked the car door and climbed into the maroon Monte Carlo. The tears broke through the dam of determination that had been in place all night at work. She let them fall freely as she drove to her sanctuary. She arrived down by the lake a few minutes later, parked, locked the doors, and headed to her favorite spot. The endless flow of tears blurred her vision as she walked. Guided by her instincts, she walked up the cement steps to the balcony that overlooked Lake Superior.

The vast sky seemed dark and empty with the moon and stars clouded over. It wouldn't have mattered if millions of stars sparkled at her or a full moon shined down on her. It would have still seemed dark to her. Her anguish blocked out all happiness. As she gazed out over the darkened water, she realized how lonely she was. More tears fell from her swollen, red-rimmed eyes as she thought about her friends and family. She knew they loved her, but sometimes it just seemed like they didn't understand her. She felt so alone and lost. Letting her face fall into her hands, she cried harder. She knew she shouldn't feel sorry for herself, but she couldn't help it. She had been carrying all this stuff with her for so long that she had finally reached her breaking point.

Shivering slightly, she wiped some of the tears away and decided to head back. She walked slowly, her sad thoughts tagging along with every step she took. Staring at the ground, the tears persistently accumulated in her eyes. Some rolled down her cheeks while others fell silently upon the damp grass. Her weak body trembled as her raging emotions took their toll on her. Finally, Mary reached her car. Her bangs hung in her eyes as she fumbled for the key to unlock the door. Before she could unlock it, a pair of hands grabbed her roughly. It happened so fast her mind couldn't register what to do. She felt light headed and weak. She couldn't make herself run or scream. It seemed as if her body refused to function.

Her body collapsed against his as he dragged her into his van. She closed her eyes and prayed fervently. *Lord, please help me. I am so sorry for getting upset about my life. Please let me live. Please give me another chance. I am so sorry.* She cried and prayed to block out the hurt and pain this evil man was causing her. *Please let me live.* She cried and cried until finally he flung open the door, threw her onto the cold, hard pavement, and sped off.

Disorientated and half-naked, Mary sat up slowly and shivered. She squinted as she tried to read the departing van's license plate, but the distance and darkness made it impossible to see. Forcing herself to her feet, she unlocked the door of her car and fell onto the seat. Her bare legs felt cold against the leather. She drove mindlessly as if on autopilot, and somehow made it back to her apartment.

She wrapped a coat around her bottom half, got into her place, and locked the door. She tore off the rest of her clothes and jumped into a hot shower. Trying to get every bit of that man off of her, she scrubbed and scrubbed. Tears fell with the water drops. She couldn't believe she still had tears to cry. She had never cried so much in her entire life. Letting the water run over her head and stream down her back, she thanked God for allowing her to live. Wrapping a warm towel around herself, she walked into her room and shut the door.

In the darkness, Mary flopped down on her bed and replayed the night's events. Sitting there in disbelief, it seemed so surreal that this could have happened to her. She just wished she had done something. She should have screamed or kicked him, but she hadn't. She had just let him do that to her. Hating herself for being so foolish and weak, she closed her eyes. A horrifying image of a man in a facemask haunted her. She needed to call someone, someone who would know what to do.

Mary reached for the phone and dialed the familiar number. "Jake?" she said when she heard someone pick up.

"Hey, Mary, what's up?" he asked.

"Nothing, I ah...I just wanted to talk. Something happened..." she broke off as the crying drowned out her words. Opening her mouth to continue, she couldn't form the words to speak. She needed to tell him though. He would know what to do since he was in the middle of his training at the police academy. He would know if she should do anything at all.

"Mary, talk to me please." Worry filled his voice. "I can't help you if I don't know what's wrong."

"Jake, tonight after work I went down by the lake to think. When I was down there, some man attacked me and…and," taking a deep breath she spit out the last words, "he raped me."

"Oh, Mary."

"I'm sorry for calling. I just didn't know what to do. Should I just forget about it and pretend it never happened? I mean, it's not like I can help the cops catch this guy. I couldn't see him at all. The only thing I know is that he drives a dark blue van. I'm so scared. I don't want anyone else to know. They'll hate me and think I'm an idiot for even going down there. I'm tired of letting people down." She rambled and cried as she talked to him.

"Mary, calm down. I'm glad you called me. I want to help you. One of my friends from high school was raped last year, and she didn't do anything about it. She told me, but she refused to speak to a counselor or the police. Now she is on anti-depressants and extremely suicidal. I'm not saying you would end up like that, but you have a high chance. It's not healthy to hold it all in. Please, Mary, at least call the cops. They will help you through it. I am so sorry this happened. I wish I could have been there to protect you."

"It's not your fault that you're five hours away. I'm just glad you answered your phone. Thank you so much for listening. I didn't know who else to call."

"Well, I'm glad you called me. You're a great friend, and I care about you a lot. I just want you to be okay. I don't want you to be ruined by this, so you need to call the police. Are you going to do it?"

"I guess. I just don't know what to do. Do I dial 911 or something else?"

Jake thought for a moment before answering her. "Actually, I know a cop in Duluth. I could give him a call if you wanted and explain what happened. He's a great guy, and he'll know what to do. I'll have to give him your cell phone number. Is that okay?"

"Yes, that's fine." She let out a huge sigh and wiped at the tears. "I greatly appreciate it, Jake. Thank you."

"No problem. I'm glad I could help. Bye, Mary."

"Bye." Curling up in a ball, she hugged a pillow to her chest and sobbed loudly. Her shoulders heaved and her body shook as her cheeks became damp again. She wanted to go to sleep, but every time she closed her eyes, she saw him. She wanted it to stop. The reality of it all hit her like a ton of bricks as the hurt grew inside of her. How could a person act like that? Why had he done this to her? Why had God let it happen? He had allowed her to live, but couldn't He have stopped it in the first place? Her unanswered questions hung in the air when her phone began to ring.

"So the cop called me and came to my apartment to take me to the hospital." Mary told him and continued to fill him in about the nurse in the emergency room, how she forgave her rapist, how hard it was to tell her family, and how she had become a stronger person.

Derek sat and stared that the incredible woman before him. He'd never known anyone with such strength. He loved her more and more with each passing moment. He wanted to know everything about her and fall even deeper in love with her. His happy feelings of love were crushed with an overpowering urge to hurt that man—no, that beast that had hurt this precious woman so deeply.

She looked at his handsome face and bit her lip. "There is something else. That night, I refused to let that man ruin my life. I turned to God and gave into Him instead of giving into bitterness or hate. I wanted to move on, and I have, except for the letters."

"Letters? What do you mean?" He wrinkled his forehead in confusion.

"Well, I've been getting letters from someone. I'm not sure whom they are from, but I think they are from the man who raped me. They first started coming around the one-year anniversary of that night. They came for a couple of weeks and then stopped. Around the same time the next year, the same thing happened. Now it is happening again—for the third year in a row. It's frustrating because the police can't do much about it because there isn't any proof except for the notes themselves. I don't know what to do. Nothing became of his threats in the past, but I'm still scared. I'm afraid that this time the notes will come true."

Derek pulled her into his lap and hugged her. "Don't be scared, Mary. I'll protect you." The thought of that man out there somewhere still hurting her made his blood boil. He kept his calm on the outside, but on the inside he wanted to scream. Maybe he could hide her somewhere so no one could hurt her. He knew the idea was ludicrous, but the thought of someone harming Mary made him sick. When she had passed out the night before, he had felt ill. His stomach churned as his mind reverted to the events of the night before. Mary had fainted because of a pair of pants. Shocked by the realization of what had happened, his mouth dropped open, and he could barely form the words to speak. "Mary, the pants...were they—"

"Yes, they were the pants I had on the night I was raped."

Maria S. Sakry

CHAPTER 16

Derek hadn't wanted to leave. He had wanted to stay with her and protect her, but she hadn't wanted him to spend the night. He knew she was right, but it bothered him that he couldn't be in control of this situation. He had even tried calling Eric to see if he could crash at his place just to be closer to Mary, but there had been no answer. The pants thing really upset him. What kind of person did that? He worried what the psycho would do next to get her attention. Would he attempt to harm her in some way? That thought made him stomp harder on the gas pedal as he drove back to his house. He couldn't bear the thought of losing her. It had taken him so long to find her; he wasn't going to give her up that easily. Determined as he was, he still knew that God was ultimately in control. Keeping his eyes on the road, he silently prayed. *Please keep her safe and show me a way to help her.* He felt his anger reside as he prayed. *Help me to remember that you alone are in control, and you have your own plan, whatever that may be.*

Mary stared out the window until she could no longer see the taillights of Derek's car. She liked him a lot. She'd never known a man so sweet and understanding. He had listened to her and comforted her through her entire story. She looked down at the small slip of paper in her hand and smiled. She knew she would keep it forever. It probably didn't seem very special to most people, but to her it was. The paper contained seven numbers scrawled in Derek's perfect handwriting. She couldn't wait to go on their date tomorrow. Her smile grew as she thought about him. She still couldn't believe that he had asked her, and that she had actually said yes. She couldn't wait to see him and talk to him again. They had become so close over the past few days. She had told him things that she hadn't shared with a lot of people.

Letting out a small sigh, she flopped onto the sofa and called Maverick over. He jumped up beside her and laid his head in her lap. She ran her fingers over his head and behind his ears as she thought about Derek. Her grandma had always said that you could judge the worth of a man by what you saw in his eyes. Looking in Derek's eyes tonight, she had seen the kind, compassionate, patient man she had been waiting for all her life. Something she saw in his gaze scared her though. His eyes had given away his secret. He loved her. Biting her nails furiously, she wondered what she should do. She hadn't wanted him to care for her so much yet. What if something happened to her? What if something happened to him?

The verse that Derek had quoted before from Philippians came to mind. She needed to stop worrying about things and start praying. Bowing her head, she softly whispered. "Lord, I am sorry for worrying so much again. Please help me through this difficult time. Please help my family, Stacey, and Derek stay strong whatever may come. I think Derek loves me, but I'm scared for him. Please keep him safe and protect him. Please transform the rapist's heart and help him change his ways. In any situation that may arise, let your will be done. Amen."

Finishing her prayer, she felt better and ready to do

something productive. Reaching for her notebook on the coffee table, she opened it up to the first blank page and wondered what she should write about her sister. She had tried two other times to come up with something, but had failed miserably. It needed to be perfect, especially if something happened to her. *Stop thinking like that*, she scolded herself. *Just write*. Putting the pen to the paper, she brainstormed some ideas about their past and began to write.

An hour later, she finished the last sentence and grinned. Reading over her work, she felt content with the end result. She knew Grace would love it. She glanced down at her watch and decided to call it a day. Dragging up the past with all those emotions involved had really taken a toll on her. Thoroughly exhausted, she fell asleep as soon as her head hit the pillow.

The gloomy, cold Tuesday morning fit Trent's mood perfectly. Nothing seemed to be going right. He had headed into the shop early to get stuff done, but halfway there the sky had decided to open up and dump water all over him. Drenched from the pouring rain, his clothes clung to him like a second skin. He walked around the garage with a scowl on his face as he tried to find the sign for the front of the shop. Since he planned to open the next day, he wanted to have the sign advertising his business all set up and looking sharp. The sign apparently had a different agenda, though, because it had gone missing.

Annoyed, he plopped down in his chair and looked around the office. Where could he have put that? It was a decently sized sign that should be easy to spot. Jumping up from his chair, he remembered where it was. He ran towards the back room and found it propped against the far wall. *Wow*, he thought to himself. *I'm really losing it.* He figured he should put it up before he misplaced it again. Looking outside, he saw gray clouds still clinging to the sky, but the rain had stopped.

He changed from his wet clothes into a pair of coveralls and headed out the door with the sign in tow. Using a sledgehammer, he diligently pounded the posts into the soft ground until the sign stood sturdily. At least one thing had gone right. As he admired his work, he looked out of the corner of his eye and saw a familiar car sitting on the side of the road. He walked closer to investigate when he saw a man squatting down by the back right tire. "Derek?"

The man turned and looked at him. "Trent! Wow, am I glad to see you. God just answered my prayer."

He stared incredulously at Derek. He was not in the mood for any God talk. "How could I possibly be an answer to prayer when I don't believe in that made-up crap?" He stood arrogantly and narrowed his emerald green eyes at him.

Derek, taking in Trent's attitude and expression, felt like a common mule in the presence of a mighty stallion. Shrugging off his rude words, he looked him straight in the eye and spoke kindly. "I am sorry. I didn't mean to offend you. I merely wanted you to know how thankful I was to see you. You see, I got a flat tire and had to pull off the road. Normally it wouldn't be a big issue since I do know how to change a flat, but when I looked in my trunk, I realized I didn't have a spare or a jack with me. I forgot to put them back in after I helped a friend move a few weeks ago. If you could please help me, I'd be truly grateful."

Stunned by his words, Trent rubbed his head and stared at him. Was this guy for real? Not only did he apologize for offending him, but he had refrained from preaching to him as well. This puzzled him; he had seen on Sunday how much Derek enjoyed church. Wasn't he supposed to tell him what a horrible person he was for not believing or that he was going to go straight to hell? There was certainly something different about this guy. Feeling guilty for his harsh words, he offered him his hand. "I'm sorry. I've had a horrible start to my day. I didn't mean to take it out on you." He explained as he helped him up. "I'd be happy to help. Let me go grab a tire and a jack."

"Thanks. I really appreciate it." Derek watched as he hurried back inside the garage. *Please help me reach him, Lord. Give me the words. I don't want to push him away.*

An hour later the tire had been changed, and the car sat in the garage. "Just about finished," Trent told him as he worked on the mirror. Stepping back, he scrutinized it and nodded his head. "It should be ready to go."

"Thanks a lot. How much do I owe you?" Derek reached in his back pocket for his leather wallet.

Trent gave him a friendly smack on the back. "Don't insult me, man. You don't owe me anything. Remember our run-in a few days ago? Now we're even." He looked at the car and laughed. "But if anything else goes wrong with this hunk of junk, I'm going to have to charge you."

"Hey, be nice. She can hear you." Derek laughed. "I'm sure I'll be back sometime though; she likes to keep me on my toes."

"Yeah, I bet."

"Well, I guess I should get going. Thanks again for everything."

"No problem. Hey, Derek?" Trent hesitated for a moment. "Can I ask you something?"

"Sure, what's up?"

So many questions floated through his mind. He wanted to know so much, but he didn't want him to think he was weird. He just didn't understand how a person could be so nice. It just didn't make sense to him. "I left church early on Sunday," he blurted out.

Amused by his confession, Derek fought the smile back. "Yeah?"

"'Yeah?' That's all you're going to say? Why aren't you pestering me with questions or yelling at me for leaving or…ugh! I don't know. And why didn't you get mad at me this morning when I snapped at you?" Frustrated, he leaned against the car and scratched his head. "I just don't understand."

"Well, I noticed you had left at the end. I wanted to introduce you to some people, but I figured you had something you had to do or somewhere else you needed to be. As far as this morning goes, I didn't need to yell at you. You were having a bad morning, and I said something you didn't want to hear. Like I said, I didn't mean to offend you. I am a Christian, and I do love God. I tend to mention Him now and again, so if those things bother you too much, you may not want to be around me. However, I will not talk about my faith unless you ask. I would love to share it with you, but only when you are ready to listen."

Trent absorbed his words and thought of something else. "So if we do hang out or whatever, you're not going to sit there and see me as this horrible sinner?"

Derek wanted to mention that every person on earth was a sinner, but he didn't want to confuse him or push him away. Knowing what to do, he simply shook his head. "No. I don't want to be your judge. I want to be your friend."

He nodded in agreement. "Okay. I can deal with that."

"Great! Here's my number. We should definitely hang out soon. Oh, and thanks—you really saved my life today. See ya around."

"No problem." Trent kept his gaze locked on Derek's car until he had backed out of the shop and pulled out onto the road. Musing over their conversation, he stroked his chin and sighed. He wanted Derek as a friend, but he still wasn't sure about all the God stuff. He had said though that he wouldn't talk about it unless Trent asked him. Like that was ever going to happen. No, he didn't need God, and God certainly didn't need him. He did need friends though, and Derek fit the bill. He couldn't help but like the guy.

He may be a Christian, but he didn't act like the ones Trent had known growing up.

When Trent had gone to church as a young boy with his father, all the people had looked down on them. Only the two of them had attended services since his mother suffered from alcoholism. Every week he had heard them whisper and had seen them judging him and his family with their hateful stares. He had hated his abusive mother, but she was his problem, not theirs. When she had passed, the same Christians that had judged them had tried to offer their condolences. Trent had screamed at them. If they had really cared, they would have tried to help her when she was alive instead of scorning her. He had made up his mind that day to never become a Christian.

He remembered his decision, but now he was confused. Derek confused him. Why did he still care and want to be his friend? Trent had told him he didn't believe in that stuff, yet he was still nice to him. He shrugged his broad shoulders and realized he still had a lot of thinking to do. After all, another friend would be nice. He hardly ever talked to Ben anymore. Maybe he should give him a call. Reaching for his cell phone, he flipped it open and hit the speed dial.

"Hello?"

"Hey, Ben, it's Trent."

"Wow, you are alive. It's been awhile. How have you been?"

"Not too bad," Trent answered with a smile. "I was just calling to see if you wanted to get together this weekend or next weekend since we haven't hung out for awhile."

"Well, next weekend is the big wedding. Grace is getting married. I think I mentioned that before, so I am busy then. This weekend we are taking Nick out for the bachelor party. You're welcome to come with us if you want, though," Ben replied.

How could he have forgotten the wedding? "Oh, no problem, we'll just catch up another time. Don't worry about it." Once they hung up, Trent leaned back in his chair and smirked. Next weekend would be the best time to surprise Mary. It hadn't been his original timing, but seeing her reaction would still be priceless. He could hardly wait.

Maria S. Sakry

CHAPTER 17

Why was everyone talking about God? He punched the air and paced. He hid it well, but it was making him crazy. Who cared about God? He definitely didn't. He needed to strike soon and show everyone that God didn't exist. Once precious Mary was gone, everyone would realize how stupid their faith was, and she would finally understand that her faith couldn't save her. He would make her pay for hurting him. He would kill her just like he had killed his own mother. Women like his mother and Mary didn't deserve to live. Women like them needed to be taught a lesson.

Mary rushed into her house Tuesday night after work and looked at the clock. It read eight fifteen. She needed to hurry and get ready. Derek was supposed to be there in fifteen minutes. Trying to balance on one foot as she slipped off her boots, she tripped over the rug and fell flat on her butt. Taking it in stride, she remained on the floor and took off the other boot. As soon as she got it off, she jumped up and ran into her room. *Oh, what should I wear?* Remembering he had said to dress warm, she grabbed her favorite pair of jeans and a brown, turtleneck sweater.

Throwing the clothes on quickly, she scooted into the bathroom, pulled a brush through her long, brown hair, and put it back in a brown ponytail holder. Then she put on some makeup and covered the black-and-blue spot around her eye the best she could. Pleased with the end product, she smiled and ran back into her room for a pair of shoes. She grabbed her brown boots and headed towards the front door. Noticing the blinking light on her answering machine that indicated she had two messages, she pushed the button and waited.

"Hey, Mary, it's Tracey. I was just calling to see how you've been. Sandra told me you're bringing some Derek guy to the wedding. Who is he? Why haven't you told me about him? I want all the details. I can't wait to see you this weekend. Call me back. Love ya. Bye."

"Mary! I'm getting married in like a week! Can you believe it? Sorry, I'm a little excited. Why aren't you answering your phone? Don't you want to talk to me? I heard you're bringing some studly man as your date. Who is he? I can't wait to meet him. Love you. Call me back, loser. Ha, just kidding, I love you. Oh, this is Grace, in case you didn't know, and you better have your dancing shoes ready for Saturday night. Bye."

Shaking her head, she couldn't help but laugh at her sisters. Sandra must have called them as soon as she found out about Derek. They were too nosy for their own good. Realizing she still had five minutes to spare, she put her boots on quickly and headed for the back door. She fed Maverick and gave him more water. The doorbell rang just as she finished up. Excited to see Derek, she raced for the front door and opened it.

Wow! He looks good, she thought as she stared at him. Dressed casually in a pair of jeans and a tan sweater, he looked gorgeous. "Hey. How are you?"

Stepping forward, he gave her a big hug. "I'm great now that I'm here with you. You look incredible."

She blushed and dropped her gaze. "Thank you, so do you."

"Thanks. Are you ready to go?"

"I am." She followed him out the door and turned to lock it. "You still haven't told me where you're taking me."

He held her hand and escorted her to the car. "That is for me to know, and for you to find out. You'll love it. I promise." He opened the door for her and helped her get in. Once she was situated, he ran around to the other side, and hopped in.

Easy conversation filled the car as they drove towards Derek's secret destination. Listening to him talk, Mary still couldn't believe she was on a real date with him. She wondered about what he had planned for the night. Why did she need to be dressed warm? Were they doing something outside? She glanced out the window. The day had started out with dreary weather, but now the stars sparkled brightly in the clear sky. They reminded her of a verse from Psalms that she had written down on a sticky note awhile back.

Derek followed her gaze and smiled. "'When I look at the night sky and see the work of your fingers—the moon and the stars you have set in place. What are mortals that you should think of us, mere humans that you should care for us?'"

Mary's mouth dropped open as she turned to look at him. "I was just thinking that."

He gave her a wink. "Great minds think alike. I actually just came across that the other night and remembered it when I saw you looking at the stars just now. It's amazing, isn't it? I mean, He created such incredible things, yet he cares for us. He loves us so much. It's just amazing to me how deep His love for us is."

"I know. I love that verse. I first read it back in high school, and I promised myself that I would always take the time to gaze at the stars and remember that such a powerful God had come to earth as a humble servant, that He cared so much for us and suffered tremendous things to save us from our sins." She smiled at him. "I can't believe that you knew that. I think I need to pinch myself to see if I am dreaming."

"If you're dreaming then I am too. Outside of my dreams, I never knew a woman like you existed." He pulled in front of a building and parked the car. Not making a move to get out, he stared at Mary.

Transfixed, Mary watched through the windshield as a man in the parking lot grabbed the woman beside him and kissed her. She wondered what it would be like for Derek to kiss her. She blushed at the thought.

Derek had also witnessed the scene. "I think she looked afraid, don't you?"

Relieved that he couldn't read her mind, she laughed. "I guess so."

"Would you be afraid if I kissed you?"

Surprised at what he implied, she turned her head and stared as his mouth. "No." The word, barely above a whisper, rolled easily off her tongue as she moved toward him. He closed the distance and kissed her inviting lips gently. *Wow*, she thought before she lost herself in him. A few seconds later, they broke apart. Mary smiled at him and blushed. "That was nice. Should we go in now?"

Derek, still lost in the moment, shook his head. "What?"

She laughed. "Are we going somewhere, or did you want to sit here all night?"

"You mean I have a choice? I choose to stay here," he teased as he pushed a stray strand of hair behind her ear.

Trembling at his touch, she blinked. "Um … ah … no, I think we should go in."

Chuckling to himself, he complied with her request and led her into the building. He watched her face light up with joy when she saw his surprise. A large rink sat directly in front of them. The freshly groomed ice called to them, begging them to skate on its smooth surface. "Are you ready?"

Nodding her head yes, she followed him to the rink. As they walked, she realized they were alone. "Is it closed? Are you sure we can be here?"

"It is, but not for us. My friend's dad owns this place. I called in a favor." He led her to a bench and told her to sit down. Reaching under the bench, he pulled out a pair of white ice skates. Each ice skate held six red roses.

She gasped and threw her arms around him. "Oh, Derek! Thank you, I love them."

He grinned and took the roses out, so she could wear the skates. Then he pulled out his hockey skates and put them on. As soon as they were both ready to go, he led her out onto the ice. She seemed kind of shaky, so he held onto her hand as they slowly glided around the ice. "Do you like it?"

"I love it. I'm not the best ice-skater, though," she admitted sheepishly. "I'm kind of a klutz."

"Well, let's see what you got. I'll race you." He took off quickly across the ice.

She moved her feet quickly as she tried to catch up to

him. Not used to being on ice, she felt herself lose her balance as she skated toward him. Her feet slipped out from underneath her, and she hit the ice with a hard thud. A ripping sound filled the arena.

No way. That did not just happen. She wished the universe would just swallow her up as she felt the cold ice on her bare skin. She looked down and saw a slight tear in the front. At least it wasn't too bad. She let out a sigh of relief; it could have been much worse.

Derek raced over to her. "Are you okay? I heard something rip. Was it your muscle?"

"Ha, I wish. Can you help me up please?"

He reached for her hand and pulled her up. Catching a glimpse of the back of her jeans, he began to laugh hysterically. "Did you just do that? That's hilarious."

"What do you mean?" she craned her neck to see the back. Her face turned red as she gaped at the huge hole in her pants. "Oh my goodness!"

"Relax, it's okay. Here, let me help." Trying not to laugh, he took off his sweater and tied it around her waist. Hanging down, it covered almost the entire hole. "There, see?"

Mary looked at Derek and then down at the sweater. She had ripped her pants wide open. Who did that on a first date? Only she would do something like that. Glancing back up at Derek, she started to laugh. "I am so sorry. I can't believe I did that."

He laughed with her. "I know, I can't believe you did either. You're hilarious. This is definitely the best date ever."

They laughed and skated around for another twenty minutes before deciding to head out. With the roses in tow, they drove back to Mary's house. Derek thought about the night and smiled. It had been a lot of fun—not to mention the most amazing kiss ever. Yep, he knew he would never forget this night as long as he lived.

He looked out of the corner of his eye at Mary and his sweater still in place. She had been so embarrassed at first. He thought it was funny, and truthfully, he thought the pants looked better now anyway. He certainly hadn't minded the view. He had tied the sweater around her as quickly as possible, but he had still seen some skin. Mary was simply amazing. Even in a ripped pair of pants, she could still look absolutely beautiful. Lost in his thoughts of Mary, he almost missed her driveway. "Oops, sorry."

She gave him a big smile and squeezed his hand. "It's okay."

He jumped out and came around to her side to let her out. He walked her up the steps and onto the porch. As soon as they reached the porch, they froze. A white envelope hung on the door and taunted them. Derek instinctively tightened his grip around Mary and reached for the letter. "Do you want me to open it?"

Pale-faced and shaking, she nodded her head yes. She watched as he ripped the envelope open and waited. Why did she have to get one tonight? One of the best nights of her life had just been ruined by one simple envelope. She braced herself for the words that would remind her that she wasn't safe. Somewhere out there, waiting to harm her again, someone still lurked.

Taking out the letter, Derek held her close and read the words. "It's very rude not to invite someone to such a public affair. Don't worry. I love weddings. I will be there."

CHAPTER 18

His note had been complete genius. He loved to give the notes an extra flair with some rhyming thrown in. He laughed to himself. This was going to be so easy. He had wanted to wait until the anniversary of their first time together, but he simply couldn't. He didn't want to wait anymore. He didn't want to risk losing her. His perfect plan had just been set into motion. Nothing could ruin it now. Nothing would get in the way. He alone would have Mary; no one else but him.

A look of pure hatred crossed his face as he thought about what he had seen tonight. He had hidden in the trees like usual to catch a glimpse of her, but he hadn't counted on seeing her with another man. He had watched the guy comfort her at the sight of the letter. He had wanted to jump out and kill him for touching his Mary. Didn't he know that she belonged to him? Since the man had kept his back to him, he couldn't identify him. He needed to find out who he was; if he didn't back off, he would be sorry.

Hearing a dog bark somewhere down the street, his thoughts turned to the other part of his plan. He smiled with glee as he pictured the scenario. He would get that stupid dog this weekend. He would watch and wait for her to leave, so he wouldn't be interrupted. He couldn't wait to see the look on her face when she found her dog. She would be so heartbroken and alone. *Alone*, he repeated the word over and over in his head. *Don't worry, Mary. You won't be alone much longer. I will take care of you.*

CHAPTER 19

Mary sat and stared mindlessly at her soda bottle at work on Thursday. She had been in a daze ever since they had found the note Tuesday night. She couldn't believe he threatened to show up at her sister's wedding. How did he even know about that? He had to be close. Derek had been so worried that he had stayed on her couch both Tuesday and Wednesday night. She had argued that she was fine, but he had stubbornly protested. Not having the energy to argue with him, she had allowed him to stay. Truthfully, she had wanted him to stay, but she still feared him getting hurt.

She sighed and rubbed her temples as she thought about the past two nights. She had woken up screaming from nightmares. Each time it had taken Derek over an hour to get her settled down. She couldn't even smile at his sweetness, though, because her thoughts were too occupied with the images from her dreams. Over and over she had watched a man in a black facemask kill Derek. The way she had seen his eyes roll back in his head sickened her. She had screamed over and over for the man to stop, but he wouldn't. Her screaming had woken her up.

She could barely look at Derek anymore. The thought of any harm falling upon him made her wince. She knew if something happened to him, she wouldn't be able to live with herself. She needed to do something to prevent this. She needed to push him away to keep him safe. Knowing it would be hard, she closed her eyes and took a deep breath. She would start today.

"Hey, Mary, how's it going?" Derek asked as he walked into the lounge. Coming up beside her, he gave her a quick kiss on the cheek and took the seat across from her.

Her cheek felt hot from his touch. How could she push away such a kind, irresistible man? A vision of his body lying on the ground made her remember why it was necessary. Forcing away the feelings she had for him, she kept her eyes down. "I'm okay."

Confused by her lack of excitement to see him, he leaned closer to her and searched her face. "You don't seem okay. Did something happen?"

"I'm okay, I promise." She lifted her eyes and gave him a small smile. "I have just been doing some thinking."

"Are you worried about tonight? I usually have poker on Thursday nights, but I can skip that and just come home with you."

"No, you don't need to do that."

"Well, how about I come over after I am done? Eric does live right next to you."

Shaking her head slowly, she looked at him with sad eyes. "I don't think that is a good idea. I think you should sleep at your own house tonight. I just need some time alone. We're moving way too fast, and I'm just not ready."

Derek's face paled. Grabbing her hand, he pleaded with her. "No, Mary. Don't do this. Don't push me away. I need you, and you need me. I want to help you and protect you. Please don't push me away."

Keeping her emotions at bay, she looked him in the

eye. "I think it would be best if we didn't see each other anymore. Don't come to my house again."

"But..." Derek sputtered as two paramedics walked in.

"We're your replacements. You two have a good night," Jim told them.

Mary got up from her chair and left Derek sitting there. She didn't care. She couldn't care. She had shut down her heart to protect him. She knew her words had hurt him, but it was the only way to keep him away from her. Maybe someday, if she lived, he would forgive her for them. Stopping in the locker room, she grabbed her things and headed for the door. As she neared it, she noticed Derek blocking her path. "Please move. We're through. I'm sorry."

"No," he softly whispered. "I won't let you throw us away. I care about you, and I know you care about me." Before he could think twice, he pulled her head towards his and kissed her.

Surprised by his actions, Mary broke the kiss and slapped him across the face. Seeing the hurt in his eyes, she pushed past him and ran out the door. Unable to deal with what she had just done, she ran past her car and onto the sidewalk. She didn't want to stop. Her mind propelled her legs to move faster. Ignoring the darkness around her, she focused on the streetlights and let them guide her as she ran. Even though she was alone, she possessed no fear. Tonight she was running away from everyone and everything. She felt invincible, as if nothing could touch her.

Her legs started to burn, so she ran faster. She could feel blisters beginning to form from her work boots, but she pushed on. She refused to give into the pain. She had a point to prove to herself. She needed to convince herself that she was strong enough to handle what was going to happen. She couldn't let anyone help her. She had to do this on her own. If that psycho man planned on hurting anyone, it was going to be her.

As her house came into view, she slowed down some. Trying to get enough air, her chest heaved heavily. She let herself in through the back gate and smiled when Maverick bounded over to greet her. Plopping down on the back steps, she wrapped her arms around the dog and hugged him. "You're all I have left, Mav. What do you think, boy, you and me against him? We'll win, right?" He barked and gave her a lick. "I hope you're right buddy." Staring out at the dark woods, she felt a shiver run down her spine. "I really hope you're right."

Shocked and hurt, Derek couldn't believe what had just happened between him and Mary. Things had been going so well. He had thought she wanted his help. As he drove towards Eric's, he wondered what had changed. He knew she didn't mean the things she said to him, not really. She had only said them to push him away. Well, he wasn't going anywhere. He would keep his distance, but nothing could keep him from that wedding. Obviously that man, whoever he was, had a plan for that night. He didn't care if Mary didn't want him there. He had been invited, so he was going.

Pulling into the driveway, he craned his neck to see into Mary's yard. Nothing looked out of the ordinary, so he climbed out of his car and glumly walked up Eric's steps. He loved poker night, but he'd rather be walking up Mary's steps. At least he had talked Trent into coming over. A night with the boys would be a good distraction. The cards might keep him occupied. He wouldn't even spend one minute, not one second, thinking about Mary.

He sauntered into the kitchen and saw the pizza box. He remembered Mary laughing over his "cooking." He shook his head—forgetting about Mary was next to impossible. Grabbing two slices of sausage pizza, he headed over to the table and took a seat next to Trent. "So you found the place okay?"

"Yeah, thanks for the invite."

"No problem. It's nice to have more people playing. That way, I have more money to take," Derek joked.

"Are you doing okay, man?" Eric questioned as he took the seat to Derek's right. "You looked a little sad or something when you came in. Is everything all right in paradise?"

Letting out a deep breath, Derek looked around the table at all his buddies and slightly turned his head. "Mary doesn't want to see me outside of work."

"What?" his friends asked all at once.

"I know. I can hardly believe it myself." He lowered his gaze and pretended to be fascinated with the slice of pizza in front of him.

"So you two have been dating? You're more than friends?" Trent asked curiously.

"Yeah, at least we were, but not anymore. Now I don't even think we're friends. She told me she didn't want me coming to her house anymore. It's just frustrating."

"Yeah." Trent couldn't believe Derek had fallen for Mary's charms as well. Why couldn't she understand that she couldn't play with a man's heart and get away with it? "Do you want to teach her a lesson?"

He looked at him sternly. "What do you mean?"

"You know, just let her know who's boss. You don't deserve to be treated this way."

He couldn't believe his ears. Did Trent actually want him to hurt Mary? This guy really needed God if he believed revenge was the best way to handle things. "I don't think you understand. I care about Mary a lot, even if she doesn't want anything to do with me. I had planned on being with her, but sometimes God has other things in mind."

Trent opened his mouth to protest, but Derek continued. "I want you to realize something about Christianity. Sometimes as a Christian, I am asked to sacrifice things, which makes sense since the entire religion is based on Jesus' incredible sacrifice. He demonstrated the greatest love possible; He gave up his life for us. We are to love others the same way He loved us. John 15. Read it, maybe then you'll understand why I would never harm Mary."

Late Thursday night, Detective Benson sat at his desk and made notes regarding a case. Taking a big swig of his coffee, he finished the cup and glanced at the clock. *One already?* he thought. I should really head home and get some sleep. He organized his things and headed for the door. The phone interrupted his movements as it rang loudly in the silent office. He reached for his cell and answered it. "Detective Benson, how may I help you?"

"Hi, this is Derek Elstrom. I am Mary's friend. We met briefly the other night."

The name jogged his memory. "Oh yes, I remember. What's the matter? Is she doing okay?"

"Well, she told me not to call you, but I am worried.

She received another letter two nights ago that said something about her sister's wedding. It's next Saturday, and I'm afraid he might show up there. She won't even talk to me anymore, and she hasn't told her family about this. I just don't want her to have to handle this on her own. Do you think you could send a cop or two undercover just to make sure it's safe? Please. I don't know what I'd do if anything happened to her." Derek paused as his voice broke.

The boy's words tugged at his heart. If the letter specifically mentioned the wedding, he should be able to send someone without it causing any problems. "Okay, I'll get someone there. I'll need the address and the time."

"Thank you so much, sir." Derek let out the breath he'd been holding and told him the information he had copied down from Mary's invitation. "Thanks again. Bye."

Benson clicked off and stared at the phone. He wanted this thing with Mary to end, but he wanted it to end safely—with his men catching the bad guy. Would the guy really show up there? He may be trying to trick them if he said it in the letter. Throwing up his hands in frustration, he stalked out of his office and locked the door. Well, if the guy did show up, they would be ready for him.

CHAPTER 20

Stacey hung up the phone and rubbed her forehead. She couldn't believe what she had just heard. *Why now?* She couldn't even enjoy the beautiful sunrise because her head pounded from all the worrying. She didn't know how to deal with this. How much help could she be if something happened? She felt a pair of arms wrap tightly around her waist.

"What's the matter, hun? Who called so early on a Friday morning?" Clint asked sweetly.

She leaned against him and shook her head. "Mary. She just ended things with Derek. I just don't understand it. They were so perfect for each other. I really thought she would give him a chance. She's pushed away a lot of men, but there was something different about him. I don't think she realizes how much he cares for her, or how much she cares for him."

"Well, maybe it's for the best. Don't worry about her. Mary's a big girl. She'll be fine." Trying to reassure her, he gently rubbed her arms.

"Yeah, you're probably right," she told him, but she didn't believe it. Who would protect Mary now? Who would keep her safe? *Only you, God, can watch over her now. She's all alone and needs your help.* She prayed and hoped everything would turn out okay.

Saturday night, Mary sighed loudly and pulled on a pair

of black pants and a purple top. She didn't feel like going dancing, but she knew the time with her sisters would be a good distraction from thinking about Derek. He had been on her mind ever since she had run away from him at the station. She missed him a lot and wondered if she had done the right thing. *Of course I did,* she thought. *I haven't needed anyone for years. I'll be just fine.* Even as she told herself that, she knew it was a lie. She couldn't admit that, though, or she might change her mind.

She forced him out of her mind as she walked into the bathroom and looked into the mirror. A beautiful woman stared back at her, but she could see the sadness that touched her eyes. Knowing she couldn't let her sisters see that, she put on a bright smile and saw the difference. She would just have to grin like a fool all night. Laughing at herself, she ran her fingers through her curled hair and added a little more makeup. She turned her head left and then right. Happy with her reflection, she turned off the light and went into the kitchen.

Maverick stretched out lazily under the oak table. "How do I look, Mav?" He barked three times and padded over to lick her outstretched hand. "Thanks, boy. Not that it matters, I guess. I have no one to impress. You're the only guy for me." He gave her another lick and headed towards the back door. "Oh, you want to go out? You have been inside a lot this week. Thanks for protecting me, boy." She let him out and watched as he raced around the yard. She normally didn't leave him out at night, but he had been cooped up quite a bit the past couple of days.

Deciding to let him have his freedom, she headed back inside and grabbed her purse and keys. The doorbell rang, and loud voices filled the air as her three sisters let themselves in. Dressed up for a night on the town, they all looked gorgeous. Swarming around her, they hugged as a group. "How are you guys? I can't believe you're actually here. It seems like it has been forever," Mary told them.

"I know. We haven't all been out together in like a year!" Tracey exclaimed.

"Yeah, since Mary is always working," Sandra put in. "I just wish we could spend the night down here. Too bad Mom needs us up at the house bright and early for dress alterations. Mary, you're lucky that your dress fits perfectly, so you can sleep in tomorrow. Stepping back, she scrutinized Mary's face. "Are you okay, Mar? You seem tired or something."

Laughing nervously, she looked at her sisters and gave them a big smile. "You know what? I'm great. It's been a long week, and I am ready for some dancing."

"That's what I like to hear. I am getting married in a week, so I only have tonight to dance it up with my favorite girls!" Grace yelled over all the giggling. "Let's get going. Mary, you're driving right? "

Nodding her head yes, she couldn't help but smile at them. They were definitely crazy at times, but she loved them. Once everyone got situated in the car, they hit the road. She glanced in the rearview mirror and noticed her eyes again. Knowing Sandra had noticed, she felt relieved that she had been able to stop the questions with a simple excuse. She needed to keep the act up, though—otherwise they would know.

"Mary? Hello? Are you listening to us?" a voice brought her thoughts to an end. Glancing over at Grace, she smiled.

"Sorry, must have been daydreaming. What were you saying?"

Grace laughed. "We were trying to ask you about Derek, but obviously you were too busy thinking about him. So what is he like? Is he good looking? Is he smart? Is he funny?"

"What is this, an interrogation? Actually I'm not sure if I'm bringing Derek to the wedding anymore. We kind of had an argument, and I told him that I didn't want to see him again outside of work. Don't worry, though. I'll be fine alone."

"What?" three voices screamed in unison.

"You pushed him away. Didn't you?" Tracey accused.

Not waiting for an answer, Sandra piped in. "Well, I guess I'll be giving Jack a call. He'll be so happy to spend the weekend with you."

Mary gritted her teeth and glared at the road. Why couldn't they mind their own business? This was supposed to be a fun night. She should have known better than to tell them about not wanting to bring Derek. Now she either had to face Derek again and beg him to come or be accompanied by Jack, a man she barely knew.

Noticing Grace's frown, she pushed her selfishness to the side and put on her best smile. "Just kidding! I really had you guys going. Derek is still coming. Don't worry, Grace. Your day will be perfect." She hated lying, but she knew she had done the right thing when she heard her sisters' laughter fill the car again. Catching Grace's eye, she smiled and gave her a wink.

Grace reached over and gave her arm a squeeze. "Thank you for coming out tonight, Mar. You always make things more fun. Derek must be one special guy to have caught your attention. I can't wait to meet him."

"Me either." *Derek.* She would have to talk to him again. Dealing with him at work was hard enough; she didn't think she could handle a whole weekend with him. What if he got the wrong idea? What if something happened to him at the wedding? She needed to stop worrying. She could worry tomorrow after her sisters left. Tonight she would forget her fears and enjoy her time with them. She promised herself to cherish every moment; she wasn't sure what tomorrow would bring.

He had waited so long for her to leave, and she finally had. Tonight was the night. The dumb mutt growled loudly as he neared the gate. He took out the pistol. Making sure the silencer was in place, he aimed and took a shot. An eerie silence filled the air as the Great Dane fell to the ground. He knelt beside the still animal and petted its head. "I'm sorry, boy, but you would have gotten in the way. I need Mary to be all alone for my plan to work." Standing up, he crept up the back steps and taped a letter to the door. She would be home soon. He couldn't wait to see her face. Hopping over the fence and into the woods, he went back to his hiding spot and lifted up the camera. He couldn't wait to add tonight's photos to his gallery.

Why wasn't she answering? Derek paced the floor like a tiger in a cage. He had tried calling Mary's just to see if she was okay, but there hadn't been any answer. What if something had happened? Should he go over there? The questions were driving him crazy. He shouldn't have called in the first place. Then he wouldn't know that she wasn't at home. Was she out with another guy? It was Saturday night. He shook the idea out of his head. He needed to do something before he lost it.

Grabbing his keys, he headed for the door. He would just take a drive. He wouldn't drive to her house, but if he happened to end up in the area, he would check up on her. Confident with his plan, he marched outside. Seconds later, he sped out of the driveway and into the night.

Mary waved to her sisters until their car disappeared around the corner. She couldn't help but smile to herself as she thought about the night. They had toasted to Grace at the beginning of the night with a single glass of wine since they had to drive later and ended up dancing for the next four hours. Her feet and legs hurt from all the dancing they had done. She hadn't danced that much in a long time. It had been a blast and exactly what she had needed to take her mind off of things. As she stood alone in the cold, night air though, her negative thoughts surfaced. She tried to ward them off, but they assaulted her one after the other. She needed to get into her safe, warm bed and have Maverick beside her.

Hurriedly walking to the back gate, she tried to ignore the amounting fears inside of her. "Maverick, come here, boy. Where are you?" She listened for his bark but heard nothing. Opening the gate, she walked into the backyard and froze. The outside light illuminated a small piece of grass. She couldn't breathe. She closed her eyes tightly and prayed that it would be all gone when she opened them again. Opening them slowly, she gasped at the sight. How could this be real? She rushed to his side and collapsed onto the wet ground. "Oh, Maverick, wake up. Please wake up. I need you."

His body remained motionless as her tears fell around him. Sobbing uncontrollably, she placed her hands over the wound. Who would do this? Why would someone shoot her dog? He had been her best friend. Now she had no one. She continued to cry as she lifted her head up. Her eyes glanced towards the woods and started to scan the area. Suddenly she stopped. Her body began to tremble as her eyes locked with those in a black facemask. Her heart pounded rapidly as it threatened to jump out of her chest. "Leave me alone!" she screamed and continued to weep. Accumulating in droves, the tears blurred her vision. By the time she could see again, the eyes had vanished.

Shaking with fear, she got to her feet and stumbled backwards towards her house. She couldn't tear her eyes away from her beloved companion. "I ... I'm so ... so ... sorry, buddy."

"Mary? What are you doing out here? Are you—" Derek's words stopped when he followed Mary's gaze. He felt sick as he looked at the bloody dog. He moved towards Mary and pulled her into his chest. "Come here. I am so sorry."

She let him hold her for a long time. Her entire body felt numb. She couldn't even speak. *This can't be real. I'm dreaming. This is just a horrible nightmare. Wake up, Mar, wake up.* It didn't work. Her dog was dead. There was nothing she could do.

Derek sat her down on the step. "Mary, we should call Detective Benson. The bullet could be a lead."

"No, you're not calling him. I don't care if the bullet could be a lead. A million people have guns. Maverick is dead. My best friend is dead," she sobbed. "Please, I don't want anyone digging inside of him."

He put his arm around her and squeezed her shoulder. "Do you have a shovel I can use? I'll bury him."

Nodding her head slightly, she pointed to the side of the house. Her dog didn't belong in the ground. He belonged in bed with her. He couldn't be gone. She just couldn't believe it. He had been so alive when she had left. She should have stayed here. She should have helped him somehow. She cried harder with each move of the shovel. Derek soon had the hole dug. She watched as he lifted up her precious Maverick and placed him in his grave.

Mary looked away and glanced towards the door. Noticing the letter for the first time, her mouth dropped open. Goosebumps formed up and down her arms. She had seen his evil eyes tonight. She knew the letter wouldn't be good news. Drawn by an unknown force, her hand reached up and pulled the white envelope off the door. Seeing Derek still busily filling in the hole, she ran her finger underneath the flap and opened it. More tears fell as she read.

> See how easily I can kill
> I don't like sharing you
> Not even with a dog
> I want you all to myself
> You are all alone now
> But not for long
> I will be coming for you very soon
> Make sure Derek stays far away
> I would hate to have to kill him too.

Rereading the letter, she gasped for air. He would kill Derek unless she did something. Shoving the letter deep in her purse, she stood up on her wobbling knees and walked stiffly over to Derek. He finished piling the rest of the dirt on and gave the grave a final pat. He looked up at her expectantly as she got closer to him. "Leave Derek," she whispered tersely.

Dumbfounded, Derek stared at her. "What? What are you talking about? Someone just killed your dog, and you want me to leave? Mary, what is going on? Let me help you. Please. I know you think we are moving too fast, but I want to help you. Please just let me stay with you." Tears filled his eyes as he pleaded with her.

She closed her eyes. Her heart ached for him. She wanted to wipe his tears away and let him comfort her, but she couldn't. She needed to do this, or he would be next. "I told you before, Derek. We are through. I don't want you, and I don't need you. Leave, Derek. Leave me alone."

He stumbled backwards as her words pierced his heart. He'd never been hurt so badly, not even by Athalia. He had only wanted to help her, but she didn't care. Maybe she never had. Maybe he had fooled himself into thinking that she had wanted to be with him. Keeping his eyes down, he stalked past her. If she wasn't going to let him protect her then there was only one thing he could do. He needed to pray.

CHAPTER 21

It's Friday already, Mary thought. Wondering what had happened to her week, she flopped down on the bed and sighed. She could barely separate one day from the next. Sleepless nights, thanks to the nightmares about Maverick and Derek, had run into long days at work. Somehow she had made it through each day, but she couldn't remember a single call she had been on. It was as if a part of her had died with Maverick. She shook her head. She couldn't keep on living this way. All she wanted was a normal life, a life where she could be safe and free to be Derek's girlfriend. Was that too much to ask?

A deep sadness settled over her as she thought about him. She hadn't seen him since Saturday night. She knew her words had hurt him immensely; Derek had even called in sick on Thursday. Rolling onto her stomach, she folded out her arms and laid her head down. He must hate her. She hated herself for what she had done. She should have shown him the letter and asked his opinion instead of just pushing him away. Bowing her head, she asked God to forgive her for her thoughtless actions. Knowing she needed to apologize to Derek next, she picked up the phone and punched in his number.

When his machine picked up, she let out an exasperated breath. "Hi, it's me, Mary, I just wanted to talk. Please call me back when you get this. Bye." Noticing the time on her cell phone, she sprang off the bed and rushed to her closet. She only had an hour until the rehearsal dinner started, and it took at least an hour to get there. She frantically threw a forest green dress over her head and pulled on a pair of matching heels. Checking her hair and makeup quickly, she shrugged. *Good enough.* She ran into the kitchen, grabbed her purse, coat, and packed bag, and headed out the door.

With the heat blasting and the radio blaring, she drove wildly towards St. Cloud. She checked her mirrors continually as she moved through the traffic. A beeping sound cut through the air. She turned the music down and picked up her phone. "Hello?"

"Mary, where are you? Are you okay?"

Disappointment hit her. She had been hoping for it to be Derek. "Yes, Sandra, I am okay. I might be ten minutes late, though. I lost track of the time. Can you cover for me? You know, stall a little bit?"

"Lost track of the time? What were you and Derek doing?" she teased.

"Ha ha, very funny. Actually he can't make it after all. I'm coming alone."

"Mary—"

"Oh, I have to go. Traffic is horrible. Bye." Not waiting for a response, Mary hung up and frowned. She wasn't in the mood to hear any dating lectures. She knew she had issues with relationships; she didn't need to be reminded all the time. Finding an opening through the cars that crowded the freeway, she hit the gas and passed them quickly. Right now she needed speed. She needed to break away and be reckless before she arrived at the dinner. Once she got there, she would have to be calm and collected. She would have to smile and laugh, when all she really wanted to do was cry.

After a long day of work, Derek unlocked his front door and stepped inside the empty house. He collapsed into his brown, leather chair and stared at the wall. There had been four accidents today. He felt rundown, both physically and emotionally. Some of the patients hadn't made it. He could still see lifeless eyes staring up at him, except the eyes he saw were Mary's, not theirs. Each patient reminded him that Mary could be next and that he might need to be prepared for such a sight. He rubbed his temples. It didn't matter how much he avoided her, she still occupied the majority of his thoughts. He cared so much for her, but she obviously didn't feel the same. After the things she had said on Saturday, he had decided it would be best to just back off and leave it to God.

He couldn't help but think about her, though. He should be with her right now at the rehearsal dinner meeting her family. He wondered what she had worn. Shaking his head, he knew it didn't matter. Mary looked beautiful in everything. *Oh, why did she say those things? God, why would you give me such an incredible love and then take it away?* He knew he shouldn't blame God, but he felt so frustrated and scared. *I'm sorry, Lord. I know your plan is perfect. Help me to trust you. Mary is in your hands. Please keep her safe.* A lone tear slid down his cheek as he finished his prayer.

Feeling drowsy, he closed his eyes and leaned his head against the cool leather. He tried to stay awake, but the recliner felt so comfortable. *I should check the machine. Maybe Eric called,* he thought right before his weary body drifted off to sleep.

"Clint! Where are you?" Stacey called up the stairs Friday

night. Only silence answered her. "Clint!" Her red heels clicked loudly as she ran up the steps to his office. Seeing him hunched over his desk with his head down, she rushed over to him and tapped his shoulder. "Clinton? Are you okay?"

He jumped awake and flung papers everywhere. "What? What are you doing up here? I'm working." He narrowed his eyes at her and frowned. "Why are you all dressed up? Where are you going?"

Ignoring his rude behavior, she stared at him. "I am going to my mom's, remember? I'll be back on Sunday. I called for you so I could say goodbye. You didn't answer, though, so I ran up here to check on you. I didn't mean to interrupt your nap."

"Oh," his face relaxed. "I guess that slipped my mind. Sorry for being so grumpy. I needed to wake up anyways, so I could finish this project. Thank you, hun." He got up from his desk and gave her a kiss. "Have fun with your mom."

"Thanks, see you later." She turned to go and walked quickly from the room. He acted stranger every day. How could a person go from rude to charming in the blink of an eye? She loved him so much, but did he truly love her? She thought people who loved each other treated each other with respect and patience. Why didn't Clint then? Why did he feel like he had to be mean to her? Did it make him feel better? Should she still marry him? *Guide me, Lord. I don't know what to do,* she thought as she headed out the door. She couldn't wait to get to her mom's. They had a lot of things to discuss.

"Wow. There she is. I can't believe I get to spend an entire weekend with such an exquisite creature," Jack whispered into Sandra's ear.

Seated to his left, Sandra couldn't help but laugh at Jack's reaction. He had a point though. The short, green dress hugged Mary's every curve and showed off her long, toned legs. Her long, brown hair hung in silky waves with a few curled tendrils framing her angelic face. Every eye in the room watched as she entered the dining room.

Mary didn't notice, though, her gaze remained fixated on Sandra. It had taken her only seconds to see the strange man sitting next to Ryan. How could her sister do that to her? Did she really think that Mary needed someone so much that she would invite that Jack guy at the last minute? This guy probably thought she was the biggest loser ever. Keeping her face neutral, she reached the table and gracefully slid into her seat between Jack and Tracey. Her eyes never left Sandra's.

Sandra inwardly cringed as she saw the daggers in Mary's eyes. Was she really that upset with her? She thought she had been doing her a favor. Didn't she want someone special in her life? Did she want to be alone forever? Sandra glanced at Jack. He practically drooled as he gawked at Mary. Mary didn't even notice. She never did. She had been oblivious to male attention as long as Sandra could remember. She should be happy that Sandra had helped her out.

Ding ding ding. James Canfield tapped his glass with his knife. "Now that we're all here," he paused and gave Mary a wink. "Would you all please bow your heads and join me in our dinner prayer? Bless us, O Lord, for these thy gifts which we are about to receive from thy bounty through Christ our Lord, Amen."

As soon as the prayer concluded, Mary watched everyone dig into the food. She couldn't, though; her appetite had disappeared. She saw Sandra and Tracey give her worried looks, but she didn't care. Avoiding their gazes, she looked toward the table where Grace sat. Looking happy and completely in love, she laughed at something Nick whispered into her ear.

Mary felt a tug at her heart. She had lost her best friend and last sister. Now all her sisters had their own families. They wouldn't need her anymore. Maybe it would be best if the guy did get her. Then her family wouldn't have to worry about her being alone anymore, especially now that Derek didn't want her. She checked her phone for the hundredth time. There still wasn't a message from him.

"Are you waiting for your boyfriend to call?" a voice broke into her pity session. She looked up at Jack and forced a smile onto her lips.

"No, I guess we haven't properly met. I'm Mary Canfield. I'm sorry about Sandra calling you at the last minute."

"Don't be. I'm not." He gave her a big grin and held out his hand. "I'm Jack Timmons. It's nice to finally meet you."

She shook his hand and looked at him for the first time all night. Dark brown eyes stared back at her. Caught off guard by his striking good looks, she blushed and let go of his hand. "It's nice to meet you too. Um, if you'll excuse me for a minute, I need to go to the bathroom." Slipping away quickly, she breathed a sigh of relief and walked out of the room. Why had he looked at her like that? It scared her. He didn't even know her. Why did her sister invite him? Didn't she realize she had enough to deal with?

Huffing loudly, she flung open the bathroom door and stepped in. She placed her hands on the porcelain sink and took a few deep breaths. She could do this. She only had to get through the next hour and tomorrow night. She would be fine.

"Mary? Are you okay? What in the world are you doing in here?" Grace asked.

Mary looked in the mirror and saw her three sisters staring back at her. "What is this, an ambush? I just needed some air."

"I told you Jack's looks were breathtaking." Sandra joked.

Mary put her head down and fought back the tears. "Why did you invite him?" she asked softly. "Did you do it because you find me pathetic since I don't have a boy-friend or a husband like you guys? Well, I'm sorry that I don't fit in."

Shocked by her words, her sisters glanced at one another, then back at Mary. Sandra stepped forward. "We would never think you are pathetic. We love you. I knew Jack had been interested in you for a while, so I thought I would invite him. I didn't mean to hurt your feelings; I just didn't want you to be alone all weekend. I'm sorry."

Grace hugged Mary tightly. "Don't ever say that you don't fit with us, because you do. You always will. Sisters always fit, no matter what. Whether you are single for-ever or marry Jack someday," she teased. "You are a part of us."

"Yep, you are stuck, missy. You will forever be a Canfield sister," Tracey added and moved towards Mary. "Group hug."

Mary sniffled and laughed. "Thanks, guys. I needed

Maria S. Sakry

that. I guess if I have to spend the weekend with a man, at least it's a handsome one." She giggled with her sisters and followed them out of the bathroom. *I just wish it were Derek.*

CHAPTER 22

Saturday morning, Mary's head pounded as the orderly world around her turned into complete and utter chaos. Hitting her shin on the dresser in her old bedroom, she cried out in pain and rolled out of bed. Her mom and three sisters stood in the large bedroom and shrieked about Grace's wedding. She groaned loudly as she stretched her long arms. "Why are you guys up so early? Some of us need our beauty sleep."

"Ha, yeah right. Not you, sleeping beauty. Get dressed, we need to leave in five minutes for the hair salon," Grace told her and gave her a kiss on the cheek.

Mary watched as they scurried out of the room and down the stairs. She couldn't help but smile. Not even her nightmares could ruin this day for her. "God, thank you for my family. I don't know what I would do without their love and silliness," she whispered as she pulled on a pair of jeans and buttoned up a white shirt. Grabbing all her things, she headed downstairs and joined the rest of her family. Everyone was wide-awake and talking loudly.

"Hey, Grace, if you know how to do the other side, then you know how to do the other side," Lucas laughed as he brought up something she had said a few years ago.

Mary joined in with his laughter. "Remember that book *If You Give a Mouse a Cookie?* Grace couldn't remember the right lines so she came up with, 'if you invite him to paint, he's gonna want to dance with the sheets.'"

"Oh, be quiet you two, or I'm gonna spaz," she laughed and pranced around the kitchen on her tiptoes.

Mary looked around at her family and felt like the luckiest person alive. She knew that no matter what happened, she'd never forget this day with them. Going into the foyer, she made a funny face at Ben and bent down to put on her shoes.

"Crazy old, how long are you going to be at the beauty parlor?" Ben asked, poking her in the side.

Shaking her head, she laughed. "I don't know, probably an hour. Why?"

He let out a whistle. "They must be miracle workers if they can make you look beautiful in an hour."

"Ha, yep the best kind," she laughed. "I heard they turned you down, though. Lazy fatties like you are lost causes in their book." Grinning, she lowered her voice. "My name is Ben. I love to eat and lie on the couch all day."

Ben laughed and his wife, Laura, joined in. "Wow, you sounded just like him."

"Snaps for Mary," Tracey's husband, Dan, added. "You guys should get going, though, or you'll never make it to pictures on time."

"Yes, honey." Tracey took the keys from him and gave him a kiss goodbye. "We'll see you at the church." She led the way to her black Ford Expedition.

"Shot gun!" Bright-eyed and glowing, Grace yelled and ran after Tracey. She climbed in the front seat and beamed at her two sisters.

Mary smiled at Sandra and rolled her eyes. "Some things never change."

"Okay, I want you two to remain alert throughout the entire thing. That includes the wedding, the reception, and the dance. This psycho could strike at any time, or he may not show up at all. Either way, I don't want to take any chances. I want this scumbag caught if he tries to harm that girl. No one is to know who you are. Is that understood?" Detective Benson instructed Craig and Sue, the two undercover cops assigned to the wedding.

They nodded their heads in affirmation. Handing them all the wedding details, he continued. "Okay, you need to be at the church by three o'clock sharp. Don't hesitate to call if you need back up. Do you have any questions?" He watched as they shook their heads. "Then you're dismissed. Good luck."

He drummed his fingers on his desk and contemplated his decision. He knew he was taking a risk by sending them there, but he hoped it was worth it. If the guy didn't show up, it wouldn't be a big deal; but if he did, he would know that he had at least done something. He knew Mary was smart and hoped that she would be aware of her surroundings at all times. It just wasn't right that a person like her had to deal with all of this. She was so young and had her whole life ahead of her. "I know you are in control, God, but sometimes it is so hard for me to understand why you allow these things to happen. Please help her and let her know she is not alone." Only silence answered his heartfelt words.

Derek watched as Mary twirled around in the white, satin gown. Her long hair swayed back and forth as she danced in the glorious ballroom. Catching his eye, she tilted her head back and laughed. "Aren't you going to dance with me? I've waited so long to dance with my husband."

Shocked, Derek's mouth fell open. "You're married? To who?"

An incredible smile spread across her face while her blue eyes sparkled with amusement. "To you, silly. Don't you remember the wedding? Come dance with me."

He couldn't believe it. He was married to Mary. Why couldn't he remember the wedding? Shrugging his shoulders, he realized he didn't care. Mary belonged to him now. He strolled out onto the dance floor and pulled her into his arms. "My Mary, I've waited so long for us to be together. I love you."

She smiled and opened her mouth to speak, but instead of words, a beeping noise escaped her lips and echoed off the walls.

Confused, he stumbled backward, tripped over his own feet, and fell to the floor with a hard thud. He opened his eyes and found himself on the floor next to his chair as his watch continued to beep. *I knew it had to be a dream,* he thought grumpily and headed towards the bathroom to shower. He couldn't believe he had fallen asleep in the chair. He must have been more tired than he thought. At least his alarm clock had been programmed to go off everyday, or he probably wouldn't have woken up at all.

He took an extra long shower and had to hurry out the door to make it to work on time. As he drove there rather quickly, he realized he'd forgotten to check the messages again. *Oh well, I'll just head over to Eric's after work,* he decided and pulled into the station. He wished he was heading up to St. Cloud after work, but at least he knew there would be a cop there to keep Mary safe. He should be the one protecting her, though. He belonged with her. He let out a huge sigh. Why did he have to have that dream? It had seemed so real. He knew no matter what happened he would never forget the way he had felt. For a moment, he had been the happiest man in the world.

Three sets of teary eyes stared at Mary as the stylist worked on her hair. Her eyes matched theirs as the tears welled up again. She knew none of them could help it, though. Grace had begun talking about Dad giving her away, and within seconds all four sisters began to cry. Mary smiled through her tears. "We're all a bunch of saps. We're crying in a beauty salon again. We do this for every wedding. Grace, you need to be happy. Tears aren't lucky at weddings."

Sniffling loudly, Grace smirked. "Then stop crying. Every time I look at you, more tears are falling. When I see you cry, I cry too—so no more crying for anyone. That is a strict order from the bride."

Chuckling, the sisters complied and Sandra changed the subject. "So, Mary, what did you think about Jack? You two looked awfully friendly all night."

Mary's cheeks blazed red as she looked down at her hands. She did have a fun time with Jack. They had laughed and talked, but something had been missing. He seemed like the perfect guy, so why didn't she feel more for him? *He's not Derek,* the thought popped into her head. She smiled as she remembered all the times they had spent together. Thinking about his kind words and sweet actions, she sighed. *Oh my goodness, I'm in love with Derek.* She jumped out of the chair as if she had been electrocuted.

"Good thing I just put the last bobby pin in, or your hair would be ruined," the stylist told her.

Not hearing the comment, she paced the room while her mind wandered. How could this have happened? She had been so careful. She couldn't have feelings for him. She told herself it was too soon, but deep down she knew that it wasn't. The reason she didn't feel more for Jack was because she had already given her heart to Derek. Should she tell him? Of course she should, but he hadn't called back yet. She should drive to the station right now and tell him. *What am I thinking? I'm in St. Cloud, and I have pictures in an hour. Maybe I should just call again and tell him how I feel, in case something happens tonight. Or I could . . .*

"Earth to Mary. Come in, Mary." Tracey grabbed her arm and brought her thoughts to a screeching halt. "What is going on? Did something happen last night between you and Jack? You just got the weirdest expression on your face."

"What? Oh no. I just need to . . . um . . . call someone. Would you guys excuse me for a minute?" Slipping out the door, she didn't notice her sisters' amused expressions.

"Do you think she really likes Jack?" Tracey whispered to Sandra.

"Well, from the look on her face, I'd say she's hooked." Sandra screeched. "I can't wait to tell Jack. He's going to be so thrilled."

Outside, Mary flipped open her cell and dialed Derek's number. "Please answer. Please answer," she chanted as she listened to it ring. Once again his machine picked up. "It's Mary again. You know you really should have given me your cell number since you never seem to answer your home telephone. I called you last night, but you never called back. I'm not sure if you got the message, or if you are simply ignoring me. I am sorry about everything.

"I should have shown you the letter I received the night Maverick was killed. I didn't want you to get hurt, so I said hurtful things and told you to leave me alone. I should have handled it differently. I didn't mean any of the things I said. I do need you in my life. You have made me the happiest I have ever been. I'm not sure what will happen tonight, but I want you to know I love you. I do. I love you.

"When you get this message, please call me back. I would love to see you tonight after you are done working. Oh yeah, you are at work. No wonder you aren't answering your phone. Ha, sorry that was kind of random. I was just thinking out loud. Okay, I'm going to stop now. Call me when you get a chance if you want. I love you. Bye." Shaking her head, she couldn't believe how unintelligent she had sounded. He would probably think she was a complete idiot. He probably wouldn't even call back. He probably had forgotten all about her. Oh well, at least she had tried. No matter what happened tonight, at least she had told Derek how she felt.

"Hey, Mary, are you ready to head to the church?" Grace asked as she came out the door.

"Yes, I'm all set." She glanced at her watch. "We only have forty minutes to get you dressed and ready for Nick. Let's get this show on the road."

Enjoying all the sights and smells, Stacey strolled through her mother's magnificent gardens Saturday morning. Spring had finally come and brought all kinds of new life to the garden. All the flowers' scents blended together into one glorious fragrance. Taking a deep breath, she couldn't help but feel happy. She and her mother had a great talk the night before about life and marriage. Her mother had been a Christian for many years, so Stacey's good news had brought tears of joy to her eyes.

Their conversation about Christianity led into a conversation about marriage and Stacey's upcoming wedding. Things her mother had said during that talk had surprised her. She had never really considered God and marriage together. Her mother had given her wise advice about choosing a spouse and told her that Christians should only marry other Christians. This posed a problem for Stacey; Clint had never shown much interest in church or God. She loved him, though, and they *were* engaged. Should she break their engagement because of God? Did God really require her to make such a huge sacrifice? When she had asked her mother these questions, she had only answered with a single word: pray.

Sitting down on the one of the wrought-iron benches, Stacey bowed her head and began to whisper a prayer that only the flowers could hear. "Lord, I am still learning about all the things that are required of me. I want to please you and be your humble servant, but I am not sure about a lot of things right now. Should I marry Clint, especially with how he has been acting lately? He said he is happy about my decision to be a Christian, but he hasn't asked me about it. I know I shouldn't be with someone who might pull me away from you. Please guide me with this—I don't know what to do.

"There is something else too. I'm confused about all this stuff that has been going on with Mary. Why didn't you stop that man three years ago? And why are you letting him hurt her again? She doesn't deserve this. She deserves a happy life with Derek. I'm sorry. I shouldn't tell you the way things should be, but I am so scared for her. I am here to help her if you need me to. Amen."

"Tonight is the night." Staring at himself in the mirror, he spoke to his reflection. "I can't wait to see her face when I show her who I am." A wicked grin covered his face. He had been waiting three long years to reveal himself to her. After all his scheming, it was finally time to act. Last weekend had only been a preview of the main event.

An evil laugh escaped his lips as he thought about her hunched over her dog. She had been completely heartbroken. She had realized how alone she was without her precious mutt. When she had locked eyes with him, he had seen the fear that could no longer be hidden. Trapped inside her own fear, she belonged to him now. No one was left to help her—not Derek, not Maverick, and especially not God. He had scared that spineless excuse for a man out of the picture, killed her dog, and tonight he would prove to her that God did not exist.

CHAPTER 23

Mary moved her jaw around as she tried to stretch out her face muscles. Her mouth still hurt from smiling so much during the wedding pictures. They had gone well, though, and the wedding had been beautiful. White roses had lined the wooden pews like a guiding path. The sun had shone through the stained-glass windows of the old, Catholic church at just the right moment and had bathed Grace and Nick in light. There had been some tears, but for the most part, it had been a happy occasion.

Smiling to herself, she turned in the floor length, sapphire gown and surveyed the reception hall. Decorated with blue-and-white tulle and lights, it looked magical. Tons of people filled the room, but she didn't notice anything out of the ordinary. She hoped nothing would go wrong tonight for Grace's sake and her family's.

Catching her eye from across the room, Jack waved and headed towards her. He gave her a big hug. "You look beautiful. You looked incredible standing up at the church. I couldn't help but imagine you in a white dress." He smiled and casually put his arm around her waist.

"Oh, thank you," she answered. What was he talking about? Why would he want to see her in a white dress, and why was he holding her around the waist? "Jack, what is going on?"

"What do you mean? Sandra told me everything. We're going to be so happy together."

"Um, Jack—"

A bell sounded throughout the hall. "If all of you could please take your seats for dinner, it is ready to be served," the headwaiter announced.

Jack escorted her to the head table and kissed her hand. "Here you go, madam. I'll see you after dinner. I can't wait to dance with you."

Dumbfounded, Mary couldn't respond. Had he lost his mind? Sandra had told him everything? What did that mean? She looked down the table at her, but she was busy talking to Ryan. Shrugging her shoulders, she looked down at her plate and silently thanked the Lord for her food. At least I don't have to eat by him, she thought.

The chicken, mashed potatoes, and green beans tasted delicious. Mary hadn't realized how famished she had been. It was all she could do to refrain from shoveling the food into her mouth. When they had brought the cake around, though, she had politely declined; she had never liked the stuff. Looking over at Grace, she smiled as she watched Nick feed her a piece of his cake.

Nick's best man, Michael, stood and clanged his glass with a fork. "If I could have everyone's attention, I would like to start the toasts. I'm not a man of many words, but the ones I do say make up for that. Nick has been like a brother to me. We've each had our ups and downs, but each of us has always been there for the other. I can still remember the day that he met Grace. After their first date, Nick came back to our apartment and told me, 'She's the one.' I, of course, told him he was crazy, but then I met her. I knew without a doubt that this lady right here deserved my best friend, so let's raise our glasses to Nick and Grace. May they have many years together filled with love and happiness."

Glasses clinked across the room while Mary's nerves clinked together inside her body. That was good. How could she beat that? What if her mind blanked in the middle? What if no one liked hers? What if Grace didn't like it? Nodding to her, Michael took his seat and cued her to stand.

Help me, Lord, she thought as she stood up in front of three hundred people. Clearing her mind of all distractions, she focused on her speech and began. "Being sisters, I have had the privilege of knowing Grace my entire life. We've had good times, bad times, funny times, and sad times, but through it all we've remained the best of friends. Tonight I would like to share a poem I wrote, entitled 'My Sister.'" Mary paused slightly and recited the piece from her heart.

God gave me
A special gift
A gift that held so much
A sister, a friend, a teacher
A love no other could touch
As my sister
You shared your opinion
That sometimes led to fights
About clothes, toys, and cleaning
And turning off the lights
As my friend
We shared
Our hopes and our fears
Talked for hours into the night
And dried each other's tears
As my teacher
You showed me

The person I could be
Your insight and wise advice
Always guided me
The love we share
As sisters
Is too incredible to compare
But the love you've found with Nick
Comes close
For that, too,
Is beautiful and rare
My sister
My dear sister
You mean the world to me
No matter
Where our journeys end
You will always be
My teacher
My sister
And friend

Mary's throat was thick with tears as she finished the last stanza of the poem. Looking at the newlyweds, she smiled with pride. "Congratulations, Grace and Nick. May God bless you and your marriage. I love you guys." Leaning over, she gave them each a hug.

Grace cried and squeezed her tightly. "Thank you, Mar. That really meant a lot to me. I love you."

"I love you, too. Don't forget me." She whispered as the tears dampened her cheeks.

"I could never forget you, silly."

Mary broke the hug and smiled through her tears. "I know. I'm just being a baby again." The sisters laughed, and Mary felt content. She hadn't messed up the speech, and Grace had loved it. Wiping away her tears, she sat back down. *Thank you, God, for helping me through that and for making it a special day for Grace.*

Stacey moved in and out of her mother's room. "I brought you some soup." Carrying the bowl in one hand, she leaned over and rubbed her mother's forehead with the other. She watched as her mother's face turned green. "You don't want it?"

Her mother shook her head and looked Stacey in the eye. "I think you should just go home. I am doing okay. I think I just need to sleep it off. You should go, so you don't catch this too."

Debating about whether or not she should go, she closed her eyes and prayed quickly. *I'm not sure what to do here. A part of me feels like I should stay, but a bigger part feels like I should go, as if there is somewhere else I need to be. Please show me what to do.* At the conclusion of her prayer, the word *go* repeated itself over and over in her head. Knowing what she needed to do, she looked back at her mother. "Okay, Mom, if you are sure, then I'll go."

"Yes, I'll be fine. I'll talk to you tomorrow. I love you."

"I love you too. Bye." Leaving the room, she walked to the guest room to grab her things. As she packed, she wondered why she needed to go. Who could need her help? *Mary?* She hadn't called at all though. Maybe she just needed to be close just in case something happened. Feeling at ease with that thought, she threw the rest of her things in her bag and headed for the front door.

Pulling into Eric's driveway, Derek kept his gaze focused

straight ahead. Refusing to even look at Mary's house, he got out of the car and kept his eyes on the ground as he walked. It certainly was bad luck to have his best friend living right next to Mary. Would he ever be able to escape her or his feelings for her? He hoped he would, or he'd end up going completely crazy.

He let himself in and found Eric sitting on the kitchen counter with a beer in his hand. "Hey, starting early tonight, or what?" Derek teased and pulled up a chair.

"Yeah. I didn't think you'd be coming over tonight since you never called me back."

"I didn't get a chance to check my messages, so I figured I would just head over here to see what you were up to tonight." Derek explained.

"Well, I planned on going out with Kyle and Andy. We're going to meet me up at Dublin's, if you want to go," he replied and took a long swig of his beer.

Derek smiled and ran his fingers through his hair. "Sure, I am up for anything that will distract me from thinking about her. Can I borrow some clothes, though? I don't really feel like going out in my work uniform."

His best friend laughed and slapped him on the back. "Yeah, no problem. As soon as you're changed, we'll head out. By the end of the night, you won't even remember who Mary is."

The fast music turned into a slow, love song. Mary watched as Jack tried to find her and winced. *Not another one.* She didn't know how many more of these she could take. Every time a slow song played, Jack had raced over to her and pulled her close. She could have sworn the DJ played all of them on purpose just to make her suffer.

Finally spotting her, Jack strode up to her and took her hand. "May I have this dance?" Not waiting for an answer, he twirled her around and then held her close to his body.

Searching the crowd, she tried to find someone who could help her escape. Grace and Nick had already left, and so had Tracey and Dan, which left Sandra. *Yeah, like she would be a lot of help.* All night she had been smiling at them as if they were going to get married next. Deciding she needed to take the situation into her own hands, she pulled away from Jack slightly and looked into his eyes. "Jack, we need to talk."

"Oh, I know. There is so much to discuss. Are you free next weekend to meet my parents?"

Surprised at his question, she paused and stared at him. "No, you don't understand. I can't be in a relationship with you. I think Sandra misunderstood. You're a great guy, but I am in love with someone else. I'm sorry. I need to go." Tugging her hand free, she ran to the head table, picked up her purse, and hurried toward the exit.

His cell phone rang. "Benson here."

"It's Sue. Mary just left, and everything is all clear. He didn't show up. It looks like it was just another false threat. Do you want us to stay here? Or follow Mary?"

Annoyed, he let out a deep breath. "No, that's it for tonight. Head out and go back to your usual posts. There wasn't any indication that he would show up at her house tonight, so we'll leave it be for now." Hanging up the phone, he slammed his fist onto the desk. He had wanted to catch that guy so badly, but the odds didn't look good. At least Mary was still safe, but for how long?

Oh, it feels good to finally be home, Stacey thought as she plunked her things down in the foyer. She looked around the dark house and wondered where Clint could have gone. Assuming he went out with a friend, she shrugged her shoulders and headed into the kitchen to make something to eat. She found a frozen pizza and put it in the oven. She knew it wasn't very healthy, but she didn't care. She was starving.

Knowing it would take at least twenty minutes to cook, she picked up her things and headed up the stairs. The drive home had been long and uneventful. She had listened to music and taken the time to relax. Her thoughts had been put on hold for a while, but now they were back in full swing. She wondered again about the need to come home tonight. It didn't make sense to her, but then again, a lot of God's plans didn't make sense to human minds. Thinking to herself, she walked into her room and tossed her duffel bag onto the bed.

She opened the bag and began to unpack. A few of the shirts she hadn't worn, so she set those aside and put the rest of her clothes into the laundry shoot. Picking up the shirts, she headed for the closet. A ray of light escaped from the partially opened closet door. *That's weird*, she thought. *Why is the light on? Clint never forgets to shut off the light. Hmm? Oh well, he must have been in a hurry.* Opening the door all the way, she headed inside.

Maria S. Sakry

CHAPTER 24

Mary impatiently checked her phone again, even though she knew there wouldn't be a missed call. She couldn't believe he hadn't tried to call yet. Glancing at the clock in her car, she shook her head. His shift had ended three hours ago. She needed to face the reality that he probably never wanted to speak to her again. She knew at he had loved her at one point, but after all the things she had said, he obviously didn't anymore.

Tempted to call him again, she put her phone in the passenger seat. *No, I'm not going to look like a desperate idiot,* she told herself. Besides, she was almost home, and she could always look over into Eric's yard to see if Derek was there. Satisfied with her plan, she turned the radio up and hit the gas pedal; she couldn't wait to get home.

Waiting for his Mary to come home, he sat at her house and watched the driveway. He couldn't believe he was going to get away with his plan. No one knew who he was, and no one would ever know. It was almost too easy. She would come home alone, and he would have her all to himself forever and ever. Lost in his thoughts of Mary, he didn't notice the car parked across the street.

His car isn't there. Disappointed, Mary frowned and pulled into her driveway. *Oh well, I guess some things aren't meant to be.* At least nothing had happened to her tonight, so maybe she would be able to catch up with him tomorrow. Maybe he had just gotten busy and hadn't gotten the message yet. Hoping that was the case, she turned off the engine and stepped out of the car. Her dress swished back and forth as she made her way to the porch. Staring at the ground, she didn't see the man descending her front steps until he stopped right in front of her.

"Well hello, Mary. It's been a long time. You're still looking as beautiful as ever." Grabbing her wrist roughly, he smirked. "I thought you would have learned your lesson about walking alone at night."

Stunned, she gaped at him. "Trent?"

Gasping, Stacey dropped the shirts and stared. Clint's suits, revealing the back of the closet wall, had been parted down the middle and pushed to the sides. How could this be real? She had to be dreaming. How could her fiancé have all those pictures of another woman? Stepping closer, she swallowed and closed her eyes. *No, it can't be.* Her heart seemed to stop as she opened her eyes and stared at Mary's face. Scanning the wall, she felt nauseous. He had taken hundreds of pictures of her. How could he do this?

She staggered out of the closet and slowly sat down on the bed. Was he obsessed enough to hurt her? Had he raped Mary? Was he going to do it again? The thoughts made her head spin. Could her fiancé really be a rapist? Dropping to her knees, she buried her face in her hands and wept. *Please, God, no. What am I going to do now? I love him. I thought he loved me.* The tears gushed out of her eyes as she felt her heart break in two. She had done everything to make him love her, but he hadn't even wanted her all along. Suddenly a thought hit her that caused a lull in the tears. If he wasn't at home, where was he? Had he gone over to Mary's?

Leaping off the bed, she grabbed her keys and ran down the steps. Maybe this was why she had needed to come home, so she could save Mary from Clint. *Please, God, let me be in time. It's hard to imagine my life without Clint, but I know it would be impossible to live without Mary. Please keep her safe until I can get there.* She jumped in her car, spun out of the driveway, and headed for Mary's.

What was he doing here after all this time? Was he the one that had been sending her the notes? Had he raped her? Mary couldn't help but wonder as she gawked at Trent.

He had definitely surprised her. He realized he needed to show her how much he loved her rather than scare her. Remembering what he had read in the book of John and what Derek had said, he softened his tone. "Aren't you going to say anything? I've waited three years to talk to you. Let's take a seat." Leading her over to the steps, he sat down and pulled her onto the cold cement. "Three years and two months ago, you broke up with me. You said it was because of my lack in faith, but I always thought it was something else. I thought I must not be good enough for you, so I have worked hard these past couple of years. My business has expanded, and I am making a lot of money, enough money to support us. I also read the Bible the other day, if that helps. I have changed, and if it means being with you, I can change even more." He stopped and searched her face.

Not knowing what to say, she looked down at her hands and sighed. "Trent...I—"

"Well, isn't that sweet. I'm afraid you won't have to

worry about that. I'll be taking care of Mary from now on," a voice interrupted her.

I know that voice. Swinging her head around, she gasped. "What are you doing in my house?"

Glaring at the two of them, Clint leaned against the open door with a gun drawn. He narrowed his eyes at her. "This really is perfect. Now I can deal with both of you. You know, Mary, you really shouldn't leave your keys lying around all the time; they might fall into the wrong hands. Did you miss me at the wedding?" He pulled out the invitation she had lost and waved it in front of her face.

Understanding hit her with a jolt. It was him. Clint was the man who had raped her. He had sent all those letters, killed Maverick, and now he had come back for her. *I need to get away.* Looking around, she tried to formulate an escape plan.

As if reading her mind, Clint pointed the gun at her head. "Don't even think about it, or I'll shoot. Both of you get inside now."

Looking him up and down, Trent determined that he was too close in size to take him down. He didn't want to risk someone getting hurt or killed, so he followed the orders and walked petulantly into the house.

Stacey reached Mary's street, but didn't drive all the way down. If he were there, she would need to be inconspicuous. Parking her car in front of a nearby house, she got out and ran swiftly to Mary's. As she drew closer, she noticed a light in the kitchen window. Creeping up to the house, she peered through the window and saw Clint holding a gun. She almost fell backward as her knees went weak. She hadn't been prepared for such a sight. *I'm engaged to a com-*

plete psycho. Forcing herself to remain calm, she quickly asked God for strength and looked again. This time she noticed Mary sitting on the sofa with a guy. They both seemed fine now, but she didn't know how long they would be. Who knew when Clint would decide to start killing people.

Keeping low to the ground, she dashed back to her car and dialed 911. Once she explained the situation to the dispatcher, she hung up and moved back to her spot beneath the window. She reached it just as a loud voice moved through the thin glass into her listening ears.

Mary sat next to Trent on the couch and tried to comprehend why Clint would do something like this. She couldn't remember hurting him in any way. Why had he wanted her to suffer?

Taking in her confused expression, Clint sneered. "What, you can't figure out why I would harm you, poor little Mary?" He laughed cruelly at her. "Think about it. Think back to before you dated Trent. Who did you go on a date with?"

Disbelief filled every feature of her face. "What? You mean when we went out for pizza after the Human Anatomy exam? That wasn't a date. We were just friends."

"I paid. Didn't that give you a hint that I liked you?" He leaned towards her and cupped her face with his hand. "I fell in love with you the first time I saw you walk into the lecture hall. You tripped over the first step and laughed at yourself. I had never seen such a beautiful smile." Pulling his hand away, he stalked across the room and began to pace. "I knew you had to be mine. I waved you over, and we started talking. It took me all semester to finally get up the courage to ask you out. When you said yes to the pizza invitation, I could have danced. I thought the feelings I had for you were mutual, but then the next week I saw you out at Grandma's Sports Bar with him." He seethed as he pointed at Trent.

"You played me for a fool, so I had to make you pay. I watched you all the time. I even started dating Stacey to get closer to you. She would always tell me what you were up to. It was so easy. Finally I had my chance. I followed you everywhere and watched you. I figured out your habits. I followed you to the lake that night, and I thought I had taught you a lesson. You made a terrible mistake, though. You forgave me and thanked God for keeping you alive. You shouldn't have done that. I knew you wouldn't really learn your lesson unless I made you suffer over and over again, just like I had suffered every time I saw you out with Trent. I sent you those letters every year and watched as you worried. This year, you were finally weak enough for me to get you again."

He moved towards them and stood in front of Trent. "Now there is only one thing in my way." Raising the gun, he pointed it directly at Trent and smiled. "I have wanted to do this for a very long time. You will never lay another hand on my Mary. She belongs to me." Just as he was about to pull the trigger, someone jumped on his back.

"No, you will never hurt anyone again!" Stacey yelled as she pulled on his arms. The gun remained up, but it moved from Trent to Mary as Stacey attempted to retrieve the gun. All of a sudden the gun went off; a body fell to the floor.

Leaving the bar early, Derek headed home. It had been

impossible to forget about Mary. He chased down three different girls that he had thought were Mary. They had looked at him like he was crazy. Maybe he was. After all, he was in love with a woman that wanted nothing to do with him. His parents had always said that when you didn't know what to do, God always did—so you might as well admit defeat and let Him do His job. Recalling their wise words as he pulled up in front of his house, he turned off the car and bowed his head. *I don't know what I'm supposed to do, Lord, but please help me through this. I thought Mary and I were meant to be together, but I guess I was wrong. All I can say is, "As you wish, God." Do with my life whatever you wish.*

Feeling a lot better, he climbed out of the car and went inside. The blinking light on his answering machine guided him towards it like a beacon for a ship. Maybe she had called. He hurried over to the phone and pushed the button.

"Hey, it's Eric. I—" Skipping to the next message, he hit the button and listened.

"Hi, it's me, Mary." He listened to the rest of the message and realized that she had called last night. Why had he fallen asleep? He could have been with her tonight. Angry with himself, he waited for the next one. "Hi, it's Mary again." He listened to her voice and smiled. Time seemed to stand still as the phrase he had just heard played over and over in his head. "She loves me." He whooped loudly and threw his fist into the air. "She really loves me." Wondering if she was still awake, he caught a glimpse of the clock and decided to chance it. She loved him, and he loved her; he couldn't wait to tell her.

"No!" Mary's scream filled the small house. Trent's body lay across her lap as blood gushed out of the wound in the middle of his chest. Looking over at Clint, she saw Stacey still clawing at him with her fingernails. Knowing she had a limited amount of time, she shook him gently. "Trent, can you hear me?"

His eyes blinked open. Wheezing, he tried to get air. "I…I am so sorry. I…I…was trying…to protect you. I…couldn't let him…hurt you. I read…that verse…that Derek told me…about. In…John…" Closing his eyes, he fought to catch his breath.

"Stay with me Trent. What verse do you mean?"

His head fell back.

"No, God, please. He's not ready yet," she pleaded as she applied pressure to his wound.

Opening his eyes slowly, he looked at her. "John 15…I read it. I…know how to…treat people now. It says…" He gasped for air and slowly continued. "I…command you…to love each…other…in the…same way…that…I love…you. And here is…how to…measure…it—the greatest…love…is…shown when…people lay…down…their lives…for…their…friends."

Tears filled Mary's eyes. "You didn't have to do that, Trent. Why did you do that?"

He looked into her eyes and answered. "I…love…you…as God…loved me. Jesus…gave…up his…life…for me, so…I gave…up…my…life…for you," his chest heaved as he forced out the words. "Thanks…to you…and Derek, I know…Jesus…died for…my…sins. Without you guys…I never…would have…found him. Thank you. He is…my savior, and now…he is…calling…me…h—home." As the last words passed through his lips, his head fell again, but this time it stayed down. Lifeless eyes stared up at her.

Taking a deep breath, she closed his eyelids and blinked her tears away. She could cry later. At the moment, she needed to focus and stay alive; she owed it to Trent. Looking up, she saw Clint throw Stacey off his back and into the wall. Her body lay motionless on the floor.

"Now I can deal with you," he spoke brusquely as he walked over to her and raised the gun again. "I wanted to give you a proper goodbye while you were still alive, but I don't want to risk anyone else interfering. Not to worry, your body will still be warm right after I kill you. Where is your God now?"

Mary closed her eyes and braced herself for the impact of the bullet. She heard the gun go off, but no pain came with it. Mystified, she opened her eyes in time to see Clint crumple to the floor. Whirling around to see where the shot had come from, she saw one cop with his weapon drawn and another standing by the door. Sitting back, she rested her head on the couch and breathed a sigh of relief. She was alive. She watched as the cops checked Clint out. Nodding their heads, she knew he was gone. It was finally over. He could never hurt her again.

His stomach dropped as he pulled onto Mary's street. He could see the flashing lights. *Please no.* She had to be all right. They loved each other. He needed to tell her. He parked as close as he could and took off running. Nearly trampling a man in her driveway, he stopped and caught his breath. "I'm sorry." The man turned around. Recognizing him, Derek flinched. This couldn't be good. "Detective Benson, what's going on? Is she okay?"

Nodding his head yes, he looked toward the ambulances parked on the street and walked into the house.

That was all the indication Derek needed. Rushing over, he found Mary standing next to a paramedic as he loaded a stretcher into the ambulance. He had never seen such a beautiful sight. Without a second of hesitation, he pulled her into his arms and hugged her tight.

She hugged him back and started to cry. "It's about time you showed up."

"I love you."

Surprised by his reply, she smiled through her tears. "I love you, too. Don't you want to know what happened?"

"Not until I do this." Lowering his head, he kissed her gently. "I love you, Mary."

"I love you back. I am so sorry about everything. I'll tell you the whole story on the way to the hospital," she explained and wiped at her eyes.

Confused, his eyes scanned her body. "Are you hurt?"

"No, but Stacey got banged up a little. She's going to be okay, but they still want to check her out." Swallowing hard, she looked him in the eye. "Trent and Clint were killed tonight, though. Clint, Stacey's fiancé, was the man who raped me."

"Oh, Mary," he hugged her again and thanked God for keeping her safe. He loved her so much and couldn't imagine life without her by his side. He still didn't understand why Trent had been there, but he knew Mary would tell him. From now on there would be no more secrets between them. He gave her one more squeeze and kissed her forehead. "I'll drive us to the hospital, then you can tell me all about it."

Maria S. Sakry

EPILOGUE

"Happy Fourth of July, Mom." Giving her a big hug, Mary scanned the large backyard. "Is everyone here already?"

Lorraine's blue eyes twinkled. "Yep, you and Derek are the last ones. The newlyweds arrived a few minutes before you."

Mary laughed at her mother's reference to Grace and Nick and smiled at Derek. She still couldn't believe how lucky she was. After Clint's death, her world had transformed from a world of terror into a world of happiness. "Are you ready for some volleyball, boys versus girls?"

He smiled confidently. "Of course I'm ready. I'll bring the salad in and be back out to join you in a minute. I think your parents should taste it to make sure it's suitable," he said as he gave her parents a subtle wink."

Shrugging her shoulders, she agreed. "Okay, I'll see you over there." She wondered why he wanted her parents to taste her boring salad but only for a second. Distracted by her sisters and brothers, she joined the game and quickly got lost in their merciless teasing.

After Mary had left to join the game, Derek had explained to her parents that the salad was a cover up to get them alone. Now he sat in the living room across from James and Lorraine Canfield. He was nervous, but he couldn't let it show. He wanted them to understand how deeply he loved their daughter. Clearing his throat, he began to speak. "There is something I want to ask you, but first I would like you to read this." He handed them the piece of paper and waited as they read.

Stuck Between a Life and a Dream

The dream comes once a week with the sound of a sleeping beauty
For her voice brings my ears into a field of roses
Where their smell is a sweet sound
A sound that smells better than a thousand roses on a warm, breezy day
Whether it is a thousand miles away or in person
I could smell the voice of a thousand roses all day
The dream comes when I close my eyes
Because I believe in memories
because that is what keeps me going
I remember those eyes that melt my heart
My heart is melting with a crush that could start a fire
My eyes will melt into a glass that
will capture a light that she brings
Capture it and never let it go
For to let it go would be to turn my
back on everything that is beautiful
The dream comes when I read the words
Because words are a connection of the mind
The words display affection
Like she belongs to me
For in my dream she does
When I read, my eyes can see the person inside
Then I realize who she is
She is my dream
My dream is that someday I wake up and no longer have to dream

He watched as they finished the last line and looked up at him. "I wrote that poem about Mary after I first met her. I know I have only known your daughter a few months, but I have never encountered anyone quite like her. I thought a woman like her could only exist in my dreams. I am lucky—I no longer have to dream about her, for my dream has become my reality. I love Mary with all my heart and will continue to love her all the days of my life. If it is okay with you, I want to marry her."

As they stared at him, tears began to fill their eyes and roll down their cheeks. They looked at each other and then back at him. Knowing their daughter would never find anyone better than the amazing man that stood before them, they nodded their heads.

"You can marry her. It would be a privilege to have you as our son," James told him and gave him a big hug. Lorraine smiled and hugged him tight.

"Thank you for making her so happy. Welcome to the family."

Derek smiled at both of them. "Thank you, but she still has to say yes." They all laughed together because they knew what her answer would be. Mary loved him, and she was going to be his wife. His smile grew bigger as it spread across his face and reached the corners of his eyes. He knew he was the luckiest man in the world.

CPSIA information can be obtained at www.ICGtesting.com
Printed in the USA
LVOW07s1946130215

427003LV00001B/46/P